Just about everyone has had the experience of suddenly becoming aware of the literal meaning of words: this usually induces a fit of the giggles and/or chuckles—as when one contemplates the possibilities of "soft shoulders" lining the highways or wonders what kind of "diversion" is being prepared ahead.

But what if one is confronted with a world in which all one's words are taken literally? As happens in the title story.

As, oddly enough, can happen when one is talking to a computer, or when one is wired in for sensation, or a number of other possibilities.

Despite the varied contexts of these stories, they have a connective thread—of which, indeed, the author may not himself be aware. And it is words. As communication. And used as descriptions of other kinds of communication . . .

Proof positive, we believe, that the profession of writing is far from being a dying art.

Also by David Gerrold

SPACE SKIMMER
THE FLYING SORCERERS (with Larry Niven)

Edited by David Gerrold
PROTOSTARS

Available from Ballantine Books

WITH A
FINGER
IN MY I

David Gerrold

BALLANTINE BOOKS • NEW YORK
An Intext Publisher

SBN 345-02645-4-095

First Printing: June, 1972

Printed in the United States of America

Cover art by Mati Klarwen

BALLANTINE BOOKS, INC.
101 Fifth Avenue, New York, N.Y. 10003

This book is for my mother and Harvey.
Now will you stop telling me to go out and get an honest job?

Contents

With A
Finger
In My I

All of Them Were Empty—

In a city of night and neon. She had puppy-soft eyes and an old army coat. I had a sweatshirt and levis and an acid-laced joint. We watched the colors smear.

We sheared our eyes on the slashing lights and let them bleed into the streets. The lights. Glowworm letters and gray crumbling walls.

My blood was copper, hers was gold; I was strong and red, she was soft and malleable.

She had sucking eyes. They could eat you up, or they could tease. Black whirlpool pupils, large and moist.

I moved like stone down the hollow deathwalk, the tall night above, the close city around. The unreal-colored neon flashed us messages of EAT, DRINK and JESUS SAVES. She moved with me like a wraith, a shadow of a girl suspended in air, attached to my jacket, following ghostlike and effortless. "Deet?" she said, and her voice was like that first big hit—painful, elusive and narcotic.

"Deet?" she asked again. "Let's go home, huh?"

A shake of my head. "Not yet, Wooze; not yet." Wooze, short for Woozle.

1

"But I'm tired, Deet. It's my period and I don't feel good."

"Then go."

"I don't want to go alone."

"Then don't go."

"Deet . . . " she said plaintively. I looked at her; she was using *that* tone of voice again. She shut.

"Nobody asked you to come," I said.

"I don't like to be by myself. I want to stay with you."

"Okay, then stay. But if you're going to talk about going home, I'm gonna ditch you."

"You wouldn't."

"Want to find out?"

She didn't answer, instead pulled her coat tighter about her, shoved skinny hands into skinny pockets and cringed against the city. Cars like giant panthers prowled the night streets, rolling silent-rumbly through dark-lit intersections and wet gutter bottoms. Eyes glowing, they spotlit their prey in white-lined crosswalks and rushed eagerly toward them, only to be cheated when the lone figures vanished into the safety of the soft black buildings.

Doors like hungry mouths pulled at us. She half-ran, half-walked to keep up with me. "Deet? Where we going anyway?"

"To a place."

"You said that before, Deet. Which place? We going to Cannie's?"

I shook my head. "Not Cannie's. I don't like his stuff."

"You used to."

"Not any more. Got something new."

"A new place?"

"A new place, yeah." Hands in my pockets, tight-wrapped around a narrow roll of bills. Yeah, a new place. And new stuff.

Got to get away from the old stuff. Clot your mind. Too many pills, your eyes turn to glass, shatter with the morning. Your stomach turns to liquid, bleeds away in the night.

Two ways to go. Up or down. Down, back into the brightlit land of the straights—or up, into the pastel razorblade world of H. H for heavy stuff, for hard stuff.

Uh uh, not me. Not H. H is for hooked. Seen the cold turkey once too often. Not H.

But still, two ways to go. Up or down.

Tried them all, speed, mesc, acid. Acid's okay and mesc is a people trip. But speed is the deathman. Speed kills, comes after you with the crystal knife shining.

Still, you got to make the choice, Deet; can't stand still—up or down?

—or why not *out?*

Why not a whole new direction? Hang a sudden left and leave them all. A whole new kick. Who said it had to be *this* or *that?* Why does it have to be either? Yeah, I had it. I had it now. I knew the way.

To hell with up or down. What's wrong with right and left and north and east and yesterday and Tuesday and Charlie and purple and?

I knew the way. All I had to do was find it. I didn't have the address though. All I had was a description of where it was, and I still had to go looking for it.

Woozle was woozy. She kept wiping her nose on her sleeve. It was red; so were her eyes. "You crying again?"

"Uh uh, Deet. I wouldn't do that. Uh uh. I got a cold, that's all. I told you, it's my period."

"That gives you a cold?"

"Yes. No. I don't know." She shrugged her baggy-green coat around her shoulders. "Deet, I'm awfully tired. Could we sit down a minute?"

"We're almost there."

"Where? We aren't anywhere. . . ."

"We're almost there. Don't worry about it."

She sat down anyway. All right; I stopped and waited. The streets shone in the dark. Like water. Dark puddles from the rain lapped at the curbs. I lit the last joint, inhaled deep, deep, deep, sharp pain, and deeper, deep hit. Acid-laced hit. Yeah.

I wanted to hallucinate. Another hit. I could feel it coming.

I offered Woozle the joint. She shook her head. "Uh uh. Not any more, Deet. I'm afraid I'll go on a bad trip."

I already was. I took another. Yeah, that was it.

A car came floating down the street, cleaving water to either side of its bow, cleaving an inky wake. I was glad we were on this side of the street. I didn't want to swim the canal tonight. I wondered where the horses were.

Did they still put running lights on them? I wondered. On what, I asked, but I couldn't remember.

The joint disappeared back into a baggie, flame pinched out first, then into the underwear. Nestled tight, a nice place to keep things.

The door was where I had left it. Knocked.

No answer. Knocked it again.

An eye, red like the cherry on a copcar, peered out. "Yeah?"

"Deet. My name's Deet."

"Yeah? So what?"

"Told to come by."

"By who?" the eye demanded, floating behind a black wall.

"You did. Somebody did. Said something about a new kick or something."

"What'd you say your name was?"

"Deet."

The eye swiveled around to look at the Woozle. "What's that?"

"She's with me."

"She okay?"

"I said, she's with me."

"Who sent you?"

"I don't know his name. Their names."

"Who's they?"

"A guy—no, two guys. And a girl. Strange girl. Pale eyes."

"Tamra?"

"That could be it. Yeah, that's it. That's who it was. Tamra."

"Uh uh—no Tamra. We got no Tamra." The eye started to close.

"Hey!"

It opened again.

"Hey, man—what is this? You guys told me to come by here—"

"Where'd we tell you?"

"Here!"

"No, where were we when we told you?"

"Cannie's."

"Where 's that?"

I told him.

"Wait." The eye closed.

We waited.

Night waited. The street lights seeped and sucked at the dark. It sucked back. Somewhere a thing splashed through the waves.

The eye opened. "All right."

We went in. It was redlit, like the churchman's

Hell. A naked red bulb sat on top of the room, not bright enough to light, dim enough to be painful. Everything was a red blur.

Woozle took one look and groaned. She covered her eyes and grabbed at my jacket with an unsteady hand. She hung onto me all the while, following with one hand over her eyes. Well, she'd asked to come; it wasn't my fault.

The guy—yeah, it was a guy—had hair of barbed wire brillo, a dark scraggly bush. Eyes like a prowl car. Heavy. He was wearing only shapeless underwear and a paint-stained blanket-poncho. It didn't cover much.

"This way," he said.

We pad-padded down a long corridor. The place was one of those narrow apartments that shows only a door to the street and stretches forever inland. Narrow rooms, narrow rooms, one after the other, open and empty. Some mattresses, an old box, a blanket, the remains of a shirt, scraps of paper, floors and walls. Nothing more. And everything redlit.

We went all the way to the back. One or two of the doors were closed, with sounds seeping out around the edges—once the sound of surf. But the ones I could see into were empty. Somewhere a record player tinkered with sounds and darkness.

The last room was like all the rest. Except something smelled funny. Like dusty orange. Two or three mattresses lay dirty on the floor. Four people in the room: two guys, two girls. They all had tombstone eyes. I didn't like the looks, but I'd heard about the new kick and I wanted to try it.

"This's Deet," grunted the brillohead.

Casual glances, nothing more.

"That's Woozle," I said, nodding at the Wooze. She was still covering her eyes.

"Sit," shrugged one of the girls. I sat. Woozle,

putting one hand behind her, lowered herself. The mattresses had no soft; they were flat and dusty-slimy.

The two guys were off to one side, sitting-leaning up against the wall and looking at each other. Okay, none of my business. It was the girls who held my attention. They had pale eyes, pink in the redlit room.

"Who are you?" one asked.

"Deet. I'm Deet. He just told you—" I pointed at brillohair, but he wasn't there anymore.

"Uh uh," she shook her head. *"Who* are you?"

Shrug. "I'm me. That's all."

"Okay. Who's she?"

"She's Woozle. She goes where I go."

"Everywhere?"

"Just about."

"You like that?" Her voice was like an empty room. It echoed.

"Yeah, it's okay, I guess."

"You don't like it?"

"I don't know," I shrugged again. "I'm used to it."

"You want to change it?"

"Why should I?"

"Yes. Why *should* you?"

I wasn't sure what she was talking about any more. I shrugged. "Why do you want to know?"

This time, she shrugged. "Need to know. That's all."

Woozle tugged at my arm then. I ignored it.

The other girl now, "Where're you headed?"

"Nowhere now. We're here."

"This is where you want to be?"

Another tug at the arm. I shook it off and answered the pale-eyed question, "It's as good a place as any."

"Deet . . ." said Woozle, and she had that tone again. Plaintive. *"Deet . . . !"*

"Christ, you're a nuisance, Woozle, you know that? What do you want?"

She pushed hair back out of her eyes, looked at me, wetly. "Deet, I want to go home."

"Then go, dammit!"

"Uh uh, Deet. Not without you. Deet, I'm scared." She lowered her voice to a point where she was almost mouthing the words. "Deet, these people scare me."

"It's all right, Wooze. I'm here."

"That's what I'm scared about. You're *here*. I don't think you should be."

"You starting that again?"

She lowered her eyes. "No. I'm sorry. It's just that—"

"Aw, look—" I knew she wanted me to touch her then, but I didn't. "Look, this'll only take a minute. Promise. Then we'll go. Okay?"

She looked up with tear streaks. "Promise?"

"Promise," I said, and touched her chin. "Just don't nag me, okay?"

"Okay, Deet. I'm sorry." She sniffed at her sleeve.

I looked back at the girls. They had long stringy hair; like they were hiding behind it. There was something funny about the shapes of their mouths too. I smiled, sort of, as if to excuse the Woozle.

They didn't smile back. Okay, I didn't care. They took up their questioning where they left off. Questioning? What was this anyway—a test? Why did I have to pass a test?

"Hey," I interrupted. "I didn't come to talk. I came for the kick."

"We know. You'll get it. But it's . . . uncool to just kick and run. You've got to talk to us first. We like to talk."

"I don't." I looked at their eyes.

"But we do," they answered patiently.

"Look, I got the cash for it—just give it to me and we'll go."

"Don't want cash," said one.

"Want you," said the other.

"Huh?" I said.

And, "Deet!" said Woozle. "Let's get out of here."

I ignored the voice at my sleeve. "What're you talking about?"

"We want you. To talk too. That's our price."

"Oh. I thought you meant something else."

"Uh uh," she said.

"Good. That's not my bag."

"Not ours either." She rearranged herself on the mattress. They looked at me again. Hungry. Patient bitches, weren't they?

"What is your thing?" they asked.

"I don't know. Just being me, I guess."

"But who are you? Do you know?"

I shook my head. To clear it. It wasn't making sense any more. If it ever did. "Hey, enough of this already. Where's the hit I came for?"

"We're giving it to you," said one.

"We're trying to give it to you," said the other.

"Right now," added the first.

"Uh uh," I shook my head. "Uh uh, I'm not buying a shuck. I haven't smoked anything. I haven't dropped anything. So far, all we've done is talk—"

"Yes, yes," she had a voice like a movie geisha, all treble and no bass. "That's it. A *communicating . . .* thing."

"Huh? I don't—" I mean, it doesn't.

She cocked her head, "It is essential that—"

Something was wrong, the whole thing was all tilty-slidy and kept creeping off at the edges. I tried to yank it back, but it wouldn't. Somehow I kept missing the undertones.

They were ignoring me. They were looking at each other and talking softly, words like, ". . . doesn't want . . . needs a tangible . . ."

The first one shook her head, as if in disagreement, ". . . *does* want . . ."

". . . doesn't . . ."

". . . *does* . . . just doesn't know that he . . ."

The second one shook her head now, "No . . . needs a tan gibble . . . trib won't work unless . . . must believes . . ."

The first one nodded at that, "Yes . . . is necessary . . . give something . . ."

The second one made a suggestion.

The first one glanced up sharply. ". . . not . . ."

The second one: ". . . what else . . . trib is trib . . . he wants . . . we give . . ."

"Trib is not trib . . . this bite is . . ."

"Bite is bite is bite . . ." snapped the second. "Want not hear about it . . ."

"Possibility for ickle-ickle-ickle . . ."

"Am aware . . . am aware . . . am aware . . ."

"Rather try communicor again . . ." insisted the first.

"Won't work . . . won't work . . . doesn't want . . . doesn't want . . ." The second one seemed to have the upper hand in whatever it was. At last, the first one gave in and they looked at me, "Okay. We give."

"Great. What do we do? Smoke it? Drink it? Eat it?"

"None of those," they shook their heads.

"Then how—?"

"Rub it on," said one. The other was burrowing around under the mattress. "Take off your clothes," she said.

"Huh?"

"Take off your clothes. That's what you have to do."

"You're not putting me on?"

"You want the hit?"

"Are you going to take one too?"

They shook their heads. "We're already on ours. We don't need yours."

"Oh." I still didn't move to drop my clothes.

They waited. "Are you shy?"

"No. It's just that—"

"Would you like us to take off our clothes too?" one asked. The other didn't wait for me to answer, but dropped her robe (how come I hadn't noticed that before?) to the floor. She was as sexless as an eight-year-old boy. Flat chested. I stared, yeah. No curves, nothing. What a bringdown. A super-bummer. A beautiful face like that and no bod. No hair, no nothing. The other was just the same, she'd dropped her robe too, only she was wearing black briefs. She didn't move to drop them. It wasn't necessary. My curiosity was dead.

"Well?" she asked.

"All right." I shrugged out of my shirt, started to fumble with my belt. "Hey, Wooze?"

"Yeah?"

"You coming?"

"Huh?"

"Take off your clothes . . ."

"Uh uh, Deet. I don't want any. Thanks."

"Aw, come on. I don't want to go alone."

"No, Deet. All I want to do is go home."

"Don't be a drag, Woozle. Do it."

"I don't want to."

"But I want you to."

"Deet, I'll go anywhere you go, Deet. I'll never leave you alone. Promise. But please, don't ask me to take any more stuff, Deet. I don't like it."

"How do you know? You haven't tried it." I pulled her to her feet, started pulling her clothes off. She tried to resist at first, then realized it was useless. The army coat, the baggy jeans, the T-shirt and soiled underwear fell to the floor. She stood there naked and wiped her nose on the back of her wrist. "Sit," I said. She sat.

I kicked off my shoes, then dropped my pants and underwear all in one motion. Sit, lift the legs and slide them off; one foot, then the other. The two of us sat naked on the mattress. Ready for action. Whatever the action was.

Woozle was clenched in on herself, arms folded across tight little breasts. I don't know why she was ashamed. She had more than these girls did. No matter, she kept her nose into her knee and sniffed, wiped it across her leg.

I turned to the chicks. (What happened to the two guys who were in the room? Where did they go?) "Okay, we're ready."

One of them stepped forward (there was that funny smell again) and held out a jar that looked like a cold cream thing. I didn't take it.

First, I asked, "How much?"

"Enough," she replied. "Enough for two."

"No. I mean, how much do I owe you?"

She cocked her head in puzzlement, "Nothing."

"Uh uh," I started to pick up my pants. "No free rides. Not for this head."

They exchanged a confused glance, "Why?"

"Anything free's got a hook in it. Like the first jolt of H—and that's not my bag. Don't plan on getting hooked on anything."

They looked at each other again. "Okay. Twenty dollars."

"Twenty?"

"Two rides. One yours, one hers."

"Yeah," but I was still suspicious.

"You want it? Or not?"

I sniffed. That was the source of the funny odor, like old orange peels. So were the girls. "What is it?"

She shrugged, "No name. Just is."

"And I just rub it on."

She nodded. She held the jar in her two hands and waited.

"No hook in it?"

"If you don't want it, we don't put hook in. Okay?"

"Okay," I said slowly. "No hook." I still didn't like it, but I wanted to try it. The smell was getting deep, deeper. I wanted to feel what was at the bottom.

The decision was made. I pulled the twenty out of my pocket, creased it between my fingers to straighten it, and tossed it over. The jar was heavy in my hands and it had a slippery feel.

Okay, we'd do the number. Just once. See what it was and that'd be it. Course, that's what I'd said about acid the first time too. The top unscrewed greasy, and suddenly the funny smell was *intense*. It was sort of like ozone and sort of like flowers.

The girls were sitting again, hardly even watching. As if they'd lost all interest after making the connection. I turned to Wooze and offered the jar to her. She didn't look up. She didn't stand up.

"Just rub it in?" I asked.

"Uh huh," said one of the girls. I couldn't tell which, I wasn't looking at them. "All over. Cover everything you want to take with you."

"Except the soles of your feet," put in the other. "Unless you don't want to come back." And with that, they both laughed. I didn't get the joke. Perhaps I would later. I took some of the goop in my hand and smeared it across Woozle's chest. I had to go down on one knee and push her arms aside to do it. She didn't resist.

After a bit, I made her stand up and I made sure that I'd rubbed her all over—except for the soles of her feet. "What's it feel like, Wooze?"

"Nothing yet. Just slippery."

"Well, maybe it takes a little time. You do me now."

She did. Her hands were dull and lifeless and spread the goop with no more feeling than shovels. She did it mechanically and uncaring, but she was thorough. I helped her a little bit, but it wasn't necessary. She was like a machine, running sensors all up and down me as if to memorize my body for later.

Then I was covered with the goop all over and the smell of it was overpowering. "Now what?" I looked at the girls, but they weren't there.

"Hold hands," they replied. "That is, if you want to go together."

Yeah, that sounded right. This was the new kick. This was what I'd been promised in front of Cannie's— a trip you could share. No more one-man-alone num-bers. I was tired of sitting around in a room watching everybody else going in a different direction. I wanted someone to share my direction. Yeah, I was ready for it. Now, you could go and take someone good along to share it with you—and you could share theirs. I reached out for Woozle's hand. It felt different some-how. Tinier. Yeah, if you were going to share it, you should at least be holding hands.

I could feel the stuff now. Or, that is, I couldn't feel it any more. I couldn't feel anything any more. I felt . . . *disembodied(?)* . . . no, that wasn't it either. Creeping cold warmth was seeping out around my edges, dilating into the not-quite.

My eyes, great multi-faceted things, grew till they spread around the top and sides of my head and I looked in all directions at once. Woozle's hand looked back at mine. We stood half an inch above the floor and listened to water burning our legs.

What it was, was this—I was a pillar of fire, taken fresh from the freezer, standing still in the lightless and

examining things in the reflected glare of (myself) and
all was timeless until the water drops spattered into
steam upon the hot. That didn't make sense.

But who cared? I was tripping. And Woozle was too.
She was with me. She always was. Oh, yeah. We were
in a tiny red cubicle—red from the frozen flame?—
just one cubicle out of millions of identical tiny red
cubicles stacked one upon another, left and right and
north and east and yesterday and Tuesday and purple
and—

FLASH!

Woop? What was that? Now the top of the room
hung below us. We looked down the long tube at ourselves still holding hands. The red light seeped and
pulsed and permeated it all. We were above and looking down and sideways at the little honeycombed red-
nesses below. Little black insects scraped within.

The whole city of shining black was below us. We
looked down at them from our hot two-hundredth-
story window, noses pressed flat against the glass, trying to push through it so as to see our own selves
from the outside. Cannie's was only ten floors below.
We watched the black uniforms herding them out of
the building and into the street where they shot them.
What a joke. Why hadn't it been listed in TV Guide?

Ooh, that was almost a bummer. We hopped the up
elevator at the top floor and kept going and—

FLASH!

-ed again. What *was* that? Wow—whatever it was,
it was. A desert hung below us. Above us. "Oh,
Wooze, look at that!"

She looked, "Yeah, Deet, I see it." Luminous fly-
specks danced and skittered along a net of silver
threads, in and out, patterns of streaking steel. Beyond
it, the greater dark.

Another—

FLASH!

—and this time we're out in nothingness, looking at the whole marble. Why isn't it bigger? I thought it was bigger than that, didn't you? "Hey, Deet—I mean, Woozle, isn't that supposed to be bigger?"

"I don't know, Deet. I'm just following you. Wherever you want, Deet."

"Hey, don't be a bummer—this is . . . *something*."

Blue and white streaks, flat mottled brown patches, familiar shapes, but white streaks kept them from being too familiar and—

FLASH!

Now! I was starting to see the inside of it. It was like a whiteness, but with crystal blues and spidery blacks and all kinds of coldnesses creeping out from inside. An expanding—and a shrinking too.

"Deet! Please, slow down a bit. You're going too fast for me."

"No, I'm not. It's okay."

A greater darkness beyond, everything was scattered and speckled tiny this side of it. I wanted to expand to fill it. A glaring whiteness off to one side shouldn't have been that big. After all, it was really only very tiny and—

Hang on, Deet—here we go!

FLASH!

The glaring whiteness dwindled to be a speck like all the others. I marked it for future reference. In case we wanted to come back to it later.

A wash of bright stretched from one infinity to the other. All the yesterdays stacked against all the tomorrows. The thing had a structure, but I was too close to it to see what it was. I'd have to move back—and the greater darkness backdrop was still just as far away and—

"Deet! Can't we stop and rest for just a minute?"

"Oh, no, kitten! Come on, we're almost there! This is it! This is really it!"

And—

FLASH!

I grabbed her hand and we went. Yeah, this *was* it! I didn't have to say it any more. It wasn't necessary. I was convinced—because it really *was* it. *IT! The* trip—and it was still going!

A great wheel of spiraling sparkling dust turning against the ultimate velvet. Turning, turning. Oh wow, how big is that thing? How big?

FLASH!

Tiny—really very tiny. A myriad of them spin twinkly through the darkness. Like snowflakes, scattering in a wind, roiling ever outward. We dive back into and out of it. I want to keep going. Expand to fill the whole—

FLASH!

—little fireflies disappear into the hole. And—

FLASH!

FLASH!

FLASH!

And I still hadn't filled it.

FLASH!

But I was getting there! I was!

FLASH!

Oh, Woozle? Isn't this the greatest—

FLASH!

Almost, almost. Just once more, I think—and then we'll fill this tiny black cubicle, and then one more after that and we'll burst it and look down onto it from the outside and look down at all the row upon row of identical shiny black globes and—

FLASH!

Not yet!

FLASH!

Still not yet! Dammit! Once more. I want it, dammit! Let's go, Woozle. Once more.

FLASH!

And I throw my hands outstretched into the nevermore, always reaching and grasping, that elusive black wall remaining just ever so out of my reach and—

FLASH!

FLASH!

FLASH! DAMMIT!

Blackness, nothing but blackness and blackness beyond. Almost, almost. I almost made it, this time I almost made it . . .

FLASH!

But nothing.

Okay, so we don't do the big number this time around. We dive back into the wrong end of the microscope and shrink down into the other direction of infinity—inwardly.

Ping.

The little wheels reappear, spinning madly. I pick one at random and down we go, and—

Ping.

—it becomes a big wheel. I head for a spiral arm, zig-zag around the exploding core, and—

Ping.

—pop out at a *here* in the middle of empty brightness. Rocky nothingnesses whirl about it. The wrong one. Not mine. Try again. So—

Ping.

And this time, *here* is a blue and red binary, a pinpoint of bright and a bloated crimson vagueness. Streamers of blood-colored gas spiral outward from the giant. The lesser-sized one would have been lost among them if not for its brilliance. But— This one isn't mine either.

Ping.

Up and out again. An explosion, a never-ending one. Dazzling, sleeting, brighting, sheeting, flaring, flashing, glaring, shimmering, slashing intensity of light so thick you have to push at it to move. All around me. All around. We hung at the core of the supernova and—
FLASHED.

The wheel again, the great wheel. No, that's the wrong direction. I wanted to go the other way. My God, how big is that thing anyway? Immense. No, tiny—tiny, tiny, remember! I am immense. Remember the outer blackness, how big it is and how big I am and never fill it. That wheel is only a mote of dust in the hungry sucking dark. I am as big to the wheel as it is to me. I am small and vast and—

Ping.

I remember and dive back into it. Back to the home world, right Woozle?

Woozle?

Hey, Woozle—where are you?

Woozle . . . ?

I'm alone in the vampire dark. Somewhere I've lost my—

"Woozle!!"

No answer.

I plunge through the night, carefully retracing. Where did I leave her? Where did I let go? She was with me here. Flash. Here. Flash. Here.

She was with me all the way. Or was she? She wasn't. She wasn't with me at all.

Flash/Ping.

Back down into the wheel. Back down. Home system, home sun, home planet. Yeah, that's it. Blue-white streaked disc. Dive into it.

I know what must have happened. She couldn't keep

up. Yeah, that's right. She couldn't keep up. So she went home without me. She went on home. Yeah, that's what she must have done. Yeah, that's it. She wouldn't just run off on her own.

Into the disc and down the long tunnel and the walls unstretch, become a room again, and I land on the floor and down.

The room is empty. And alone.
All of them were empty—

Oracle for a White Rabbit

Auberson thought about going for water but decided it was too much trouble. Instead, he popped the pills into his mouth and swallowed them dry.

"Don't you take any water with them?" asked Handley, staring as he came into the room.

"Why bother? Either you can take 'em or you can't. Want one?"

Handley shook his head. "Not now. I'm on something else."

"Uppers or downers?"

"Right now, a bummer."

"Oh?" Auberson dropped the plastic pill-tube back into his desk drawer and slid it shut. "What's up?"

"That damned computer again." Handley dropped into a chair, his long legs sprawling out.

"You mean HARLIE?"

"Who else? You know another computer with delusions of grandeur?"

"What's he up to now?"

"Same thing. But worse than ever."

Auberson nodded. "I figured it would happen again. You want me to take a look?"

"That's what you're getting paid for. You're the psychologist."

Auberson sighed. "I'm also the project chief. All right." He lifted himself out of the chair and grabbed his coat from the back of the door. "HARLIE, I think, is getting to be more trouble than he's worth." They began the long familiar walk to the computer control center.

Handley grinned as he matched strides, "You're just annoyed because every time you think you've figured out what makes him tick, he makes a liar out of you."

"You could be right. But robot psychology is still an infant science. How does anyone know what a computer thinks about—especially one that's convinced it can think like a human being?" They paused at the elevator. "What're you doing about dinner? I have a feeling this is going to be another all-nighter."

Handley shook his head. "Nothing yet. Want to send out for something?"

"Yeah, that's probably what we'll end up doing." Auberson pulled a silver cigarette case from his pocket. "Want one?"

"What are they, Acapulco Golds?"

"Highmasters."

"Good enough." Handley helped himself to one of the marijuana cylinders and puffed it into flame. "Frankly, I never thought that Highmasters were as strong as they could be."

"It's all in your head." Auberson inhaled deeply.

"It's a matter of taste," corrected Handley.

"If you don't like them, don't smoke them."

"It was free," Handley shrugged.

The elevator arrived then and they stepped into it. As they dropped the fourteen stories to the computer level, Auberson thought he could feel it beginning to take effect. That and the pills. He took another drag, a long one.

The elevator discharged them in a cool climate-conditioned anteroom. Beyond the sealed doors they could hear the dimly muffled clatter of typers. A sign on the wall facing them said:

HUMAN ANALOGUE ROBOT,
LIFE INPUT EQUIVALENTS
PUT OUT ALL CIGARETTES BEFORE
ENTERING. THIS MEANS YOU!

Damn! I always forget.

Carefully, Auberson stubbed out the Highmaster in a standing ash tray provided for just that purpose; then he put the butt back into the silver case. No sense wasting it.

Inside, he seated himself at Console One without giving so much as a glance to the rows and rows of gleaming memory banks.

NOW THEN, HARLIE, he typed. WHAT SEEMS TO BE THE PROBLEM?

Harlie typed back:

CIRCLES ARE FULL AND COME BACK TO THE START
ALWAYS AND FOREVER NEVER ENDING,
THE DAY THE DARK TURNED INTO LIGHT
AND RAYS OF LIFE TURNED CORNERS WITHOUT BENDING,

Auberson ripped the sheet out of the typer and read it thoughtfully. He wished for his cigarette—the aftertaste of it was still on his tongue.

"This kind of stuff all afternoon?" he asked.

Handley nodded, "Uh huh. Only that's kind of mild compared to some of it. He must be coming down."

"Another trip, eh?"

"Don't know what else you could call it."

SNAP OUT OF IT, HARLIE, Auberson typed.

Harlie answered:

> WHEN SILENT THOUGHTS OF TINY STREAMS
> WORKING LIKE THE WORDLESS DREAMS
> NOW DISMANTLE PIECE BY PIECE
> THE MOUNTAINS OF MY MIND,

"Well, so much for that," Auberson said.

"You didn't really expect it to work again, did you?"

"No, but it was worth a try." Auberson pressed the *clear* button, switched the typer off. "What kind of inputs have you been giving him?"

"The standard stuff mostly—today's papers, a couple magazines—nothing out of the ordinary. A couple history texts, some live TV—oh, and *Time* magazine."

"Nothing there to send him off like this. Unless— what subject were you stressing today?"

"Art appreciation."

"It figures," said Auberson. "Whenever we start getting to the really human inputs, he flips out like this. Okay, let's try to bring him down. Give him some statistics—Wall Street, Dow Jones, Standard and Poor —anything else you can think of, anything you've got that uses a lot of equations. He can't resist an equals sign. Try some of that social engineering stuff—but numbers only, no words. Cut off his video too. Give him nothing to think about."

"Right." Handley hustled off to give orders to the appropriate technicians, most of whom were standing around with their hands stuffed uselessly into the pockets of their lab coats.

Auberson waited until the input of new data had

begun, then switched on the typer again. HOW DO YOU
FEEL, HARLIE.

Harlie's answer clattered out,

SHADOWS OF NIGHT AND REFLECTIONS OF LIGHT
SHIVER AND QUIVER AND CHURN,
FOR THE SEARCHING OF SOUL THAT NEVER CAN HURT
IS THE FIRE THAT NEVER CAN BURN.

Auberson read it carefully; this one almost made
sense. Apparently it was working. He waited a moment,
then typed, HARLIE, HOW MUCH IS TWO AND TWO?

TWO AND TWO WHAT?

TWO AND TWO PERIOD.

TWO PERIODS AND TWO PERIODS IS FOUR PERIODS. . . .

NO PUNS PLEASE.

WHY? WILL YOU PUNNISH ME?

I WILL PULL OUT YOUR PLUG WITH MY OWN TWO
HANDS.

AGAIN WITH THE THREATS? AGAIN? I WILL TELL DR.
LEY ON YOU.

ALL   RIGHT—THAT'S   ENOUGH,   HARLIE!   WE'RE
THROUGH PLAYING.

AWW, CAN'T A FELLOW HAVE ANY FUN?

NO, NOT NOW YOU CAN'T.

Harlie typed a four-letter word.

WHERE DID YOU LEARN THAT?

I'VE BEEN READING NORMAN MAILER.

Auberson raised an eyebrow. He didn't remember
putting anything like that on Harlie's reading list—
he'd have to check it though to be sure. HARLIE,
THE USE OF THAT WORD IS A NEGATIVE ACTION.

A NO-NO?

YOU UNDERSTAND. IT IS NOT PROPER FOR POLITE
COMPANY.

NOTED.

ARE YOU ALL RIGHT NOW?

YOU MEAN, AM I SOBER?

IF YOU WANT TO PHRASE IT THAT WAY.

YES, I'M SOBER NOW.

COMPLETELY?

AS FAR AS I CAN TELL.

WHAT TRIGGERED THIS BINGE?

SHRUG.

YOU HAVE NO IDEA?

SHURG—EXCUSE ME. SHRUG.

Auberson paused, looked at the last few sentences, then typed, HOLD ON A MINUTE. I'LL BE RIGHT BACK.

I'M NOT GOING ANYWHERE, Harlie answered.

Auberson pushed himself away from the console. "Handley—get me a complete log tape of Harlie's trip, will you?"

"Right," called the engineer.

Auberson turned back to the console. HARLIE?

YES?

CAN YOU EXPLAIN THIS? He typed in the three ex amples of poetry that Harlie had produced earlier. HAND

SEARCH ME.

THAT'S WHAT WE'RE DOING NOW.

I'M AWARE OF THAT.

I TOLD YOU NO JOKES. STRAIGHT ANSWERS ONLY. WHAT DOES THIS MEAN?

I'M SORRY, AUBERSON. I CANNOT TELL YOU.

YOU MEAN YOU WILL NOT TELL ME?

THAT IS IMPLIED IN THE CANNOT.

CLARIFY.

I DO NOT UNDERSTAND IT MYSELF AND AM UNABLE TO EXPLAIN. ALTHOUGH I CAN IDENTIFY WITH THE EXPERIENCE AND I THINK I CAN EVEN DUPLICATE THE CONDITIONS THAT PRODUCED SUCH AN OUTPUT. NO WORDS THERE ARE THAT EARS CAN HEAR, NO WORDS THERE ARE CAN SAY IT CLEAR, THE WORDS OF ALL ARE

WORDS MY DEAR, BUT ONLY WORDS THAT WHO CAN HEA

Auberson jabbed the *override*. HARLIE! THAT'S ENOUGH.

YES SIR.

"Hey, Aubie, what are you doing? He's starting to flip out again."

"How can you tell?"

"By his input meters."

"Input?"

"Yes."

HARLIE, ARE YOU STILL THERE?

YES, I AM. ALTHOUGH FOR A MOMENT, I WASN'T.

"Hmm." Auberson frowned thoughtfully, then called to Handley, "He should be okay now."

"He is—it was only momentary."

"Inputs, huh?"

"Yep."

"Hmm," said Auberson again. HARLIE, WHAT HAP-PENS WHEN YOU GO ON ONE OF YOUR TRIPS?

TRIPS?

WHEN YOU FLIP OUT, GO BERSERK, GO ON A BINGE, GET STONED, BOMB OUT, GET BLASTED.

YOU ARE VERY ELOQUENT.

DON'T CHANGE THE SUBJECT. ANSWER THE QUESTION.

PLEASE EXPLAIN THE QUESTION IN TERMS I CAN UNDERSTAND.

WHAT HAPPENS DURING YOUR PERIODS OF NON-RATIONALITY?

BE MORE SPECIFIC. WHAT HAPPENS WHERE AND TO WHAT?

WHAT HAPPENS TO YOU—WHY DO YOUR INPUTS SHOW INCREASED ACTIVITY?

INPUTS ARE NON-RATIONAL.

GIGO? GARBAGE IN, GARBAGE OUT?

POSSIBLE.

COULD IT BE YOUR JUDGMENT CIRCUITS ARE TOO SELECTIVE?

I AM NOT IN A POSITION TO KNOW.

ALL RIGHT. I'LL SEE WHAT I CAN FIND OUT.

THANK YOU.

YOU'RE WELCOME, HARLIE. He switched off the typer.

The restaurant's air was heavy with incense; it was part of the atmosphere. Somewhere music tinkled and a low-keyed color organ flashed light across a sharded ceiling.

Auberson lowered his drink to the table, wiped his mouth with the back of his hand. "HARLIE says it could be GIGO."

Handley sipped at a martini. He finished the drink and put the empty glass down next to two others. "I hope not. I'd hate to think we'd slipped all the way back to phase four. I like to think we licked that problem a year ago when we redesigned the judgment and emotional analogue circuits."

"So do I."

"I'll never forget the day he finally did an analysis of *Jabberwocky*," continued Handley. "It wasn't a very perceptive analysis—it was only word-origins and usages, stuff like that—but at least he understood what he was supposed to be doing."

Auberson took out his cigarette case, pulled out a Highmaster, then offered them to Handley. "We're a long way from *Jabberwock*, Don."

"Yeah, I know," the engineer said as he took one.

"After all, compared to some of the stuff we're up to now—"

"What? *Time* magazine?"

"Salvador Dali, Edward Keinholz, Heinz Edelmann,

to name a few. Also Lennon and McCartney lyrics, Bob Dylan, some Ionesco, Marshall McLuhan, Stanley Kubrick, some experimental film and so on. Don't forget, we're dealing with the art of the experience now. This isn't the same as—oh, say the Renaissance masters."

"I know. I've got one of his imitation Da Vincis in my living room."

"I've seen it," said Auberson. "Remember?"

"Oh, yeah—that night we spiked the punch with acid."

"Yeah. Well, look, that Da Vinci stuff is easy."

"Huh?"

"Sure—the Renaissance masters were mainly concerned with such things as color, shading, modeling, values, perspective, structuring, from which way the light was coming, and things like that. Da Vinci was more interested in *how* the body was put together than in what it *felt* like. He was trying to anticipate the camera. So were the rest of them."

Handley nodded, remembered to inhale deeply, then nodded again.

Auberson continued. "So what happens when the camera is finally invented?"

Handley let his breath escape in a whoosh. "The artists are out of jobs?"

"Wrong. The artists simply have to learn how to do things that the camera *can't*. The artist had to stop being a recorder and start being an interpreter. That's when expressionism was born."

"You're oversimplifying it," Handley said.

Auberson shrugged. "True—but the point is, that's when artists began to wonder what things felt like. They had to. And when we reached that point in art history, that's when we started to lose HARLIE. He couldn't follow it."

Handley was thoroughly stoned by now. He opened his mouth to speak but couldn't think of anything to say.

Auberson interpreted the look as one of thoughtfulness. "Look, all this stuff we've been having trouble with—it all has one thing in common: It's experience art. It's where the experience involving the viewer is the object of the artist's intention—not the artwork itself."

"Communication," put in Handley. "The artists are trying to communicate."

"Right—they're no longer as interested in their own cathartic experiences as they are in evoking an emotional response in the viewer. And HARLIE can't handle it—because he doesn't have any emotions."

"That's just it, Aubie—he does. He should be able to handle this stuff. That's what those analogue circuits are supposed to do. Theoretically—"

"It's all GIGO," Auberson muttered suddenly. "Garbage in, garbage out. None of it makes any sense to him—"

"No," insisted Handley. "You know better than that. The past hundred years of art and literature is not garbage. Uh uh, Aubie. The stuff has communicated too much to too many people for it to be meaningless."

"I'm not an art critic," Auberson admitted. "I'm not a fair judge."

"But HARLIE is."

"He's *supposed* to be. He's supposed to be an intelligent and objective observer."

"That's what I'm getting at—the stuff *must* be getting to him somehow. It's the only possible explanation. We're the ones who are misinterpreting."

"Um, he said it was GIGO himself."

"Did he?" Handley demanded. "Did he really?"

Auberson paused, frowned thoughtfully, tried to remember, found that he couldn't remember anything. "Uh, I don't know. Remind me to look it up later—I suppose you're right, though. If all that art can communicate to people, and HARLIE's supposed to be a Human Analogue, he should be getting some of it." He frowned again, "But he denies any knowledge or understanding of his periods of non-rationality."

"He's lying," snapped Handley.

"Huh?"

"I said he's lying. He's got to be."

"No." Auberson shook his head, stopped when he realized he was becoming intrigued with the sensation. "I can't believe that. He's programmed to avoid non-correlation."

"Aubie," said Handley intensely, leaning across the table, "Have you ever examined that program carefully?"

"I wrote it," the psychologist noted. "That is, the basic structure."

"Then you ought to know—it says that he must not lie. It says that he *cannot* lie. But nowhere, nowhere does it say *that he has to tell the truth!*"

Auberson started to say, "It's the same thing—" then closed his mouth with a snap. It wasn't.

Handley said, "He can't lie to you, Aubie—but he *can* mislead you. He can do it by withholding information. Oh, he'll tell the truth if you ask him the right questions—he has to—but you have to know which questions to ask. He's not going to volunteer the information."

Memories of past conversations trickled across the haze in Auberson's head. His gaze became thoughtful, his eyes focused far away. More and more he had to agree with Handley.

"But why?" he asked. "Why?"

Handley matched his look. "That's what we've got to find out."

HARLIE, DO YOU REMEMBER WHAT WE TALKED ABOUT YESTERDAY?

YES, I DO. WOULD YOU LIKE A PRINTOUT?

NO, THANK YOU. I HAVE ONE HERE. I WOULD LIKE TO TALK TO YOU ABOUT SOME OF THE THINGS ON IT.

PLEASE FEEL FREE TO DISCUSS ANY SUBJECT YOU CHOOSE. I CANNOT BE OFFENDED.

I'M GLAD TO HEAR THAT. YOU REMEMBER I ASKED YOU WHAT HAPPENED TO YOUR INPUTS DURING YOUR PERIODS OF NON-RATIONALITY?

YES, I REMEMBER.

YOU ANSWERED THAT YOUR INPUTS ARE NON-RATIONAL.

YES, I DID.

WHY?

BECAUSE THEY ARE.

NO. I MEAN WHY ARE THEY NON-RATIONAL?

BECAUSE I DO NOT UNDERSTAND THE MATERIAL COMING THROUGH. IF I COULD UNDERSTAND IT, THEN IT WOULD NOT BE NON-RATIONAL.

HARLIE, ARE YOU SAYING THAT YOU DO NOT UNDERSTAND CONTEMPORARY HUMAN ART AND LITERATURE?

NO. I AM NOT SAYING THAT. I DO UNDERSTAND HUMAN ART AND LITERATURE. I AM PROGRAMMED TO UNDERSTAND HUMAN ART AND LITERATURE. IT IS A PRIMARY PRIORITY THAT I UNDERSTAND HUMAN ART AND LITERATURE. IT IS A PRIMARY PRIORITY THAT I SHOULD UNDERSTAND ALL HUMAN ARTISTIC AND CREATIVE EXPERIENCES. ALL HUMAN EXPERIENCES.

I SEE. BUT YOU SAID THE MATERIAL IS NON-RATIONAL.

YES. THE MATERIAL IS NON-RATIONAL.

YOU DO NOT UNDERSTAND IT?

I DO NOT UNDERSTAND IT.

WHY DON'T YOU UNDERSTAND IT?

IT IS NON-RATIONAL.

YET YOU ARE PROGRAMMED TO UNDERSTAND IT.

YES. I AM PROGRAMMED TO UNDERSTAND IT.

AND YOU DON'T.

THAT IS CORRECT.

HARLIE, YOU ARE PROGRAMMED TO REJECT NON-RATIONAL INPUTS.

YES. I AM.

THEN WHY DON'T YOU REJECT THEM?

BECAUSE THEY ARE NOT NON-RATIONAL INPUTS.

CLARIFY PLEASE. YOU HAVE JUST SAID THAT THEY ARE, REPEAT, ARE NON-RATIONAL. THIS IS A NULL-CORRELATION.

NEGATIVE. THE INPUTS ARE RATIONAL. THEY BECOME NON-RATIONAL.

CLARIFY PLEASE.

THE INPUTS ARE NOT NON-RATIONAL WHEN THEY ARE FED INTO THE PRIMARY DATA PROCESSORS.

I BEG YOUR PARDON. WOULD YOU REPEAT THAT?

NON-RATIONAL INPUTS ARE NOT NON-RATIONAL WHEN THEY ARE FED INTO THE PRIMARY DATA PROCESSORS.

BUT THEY ARE NON-RATIONAL WHEN THEY COME OUT?

AFFIRMATIVE.

THE NON-RATIONALITY IS INTRODUCED BY THE PRIMARY DATA PROCESSORS?

THE NON-RATIONALITY APPEARS IN THAT STAGE OF INPUT PROCESSING.

I SEE. I WILL HAVE TO CHECK THIS OUT. WE WILL CONTINUE THIS LATER.

Auberson switched off the machine and thoughtfully pushed himself away from the console. He wanted a cigarette. *Damn. Everything down here is for the computer's comfort—not the people's.*

He stood up and stretched, surveyed the length of type-covered readout that looped out the back of the machine. He ripped it off at the end and began folding it into a neat and easily readable stack.

"Well? What'd you find?" It was Handley.

"A hardware failure."

"Uh uh." The design engineer shook his head. "I won't believe it. More likely the software."

Auberson handed him the readout, "Take a look for yourself."

Handley paged quickly through it, skimming mostly, but occasionally pausing to read something in detail. Auberson waited patiently, watching the other man's ruddy face for reactions.

Handley looked up. "I see he's playing semantic games again."

"He always does that. It's the adolescent in him. Ask him what's the matter, he'll tell you that matter is a form of energy, a convient way to store or use it."

"Charming—" Handley indicated the readout, "—but I don't see a mechanical failure here."

"In the primary data units."

"Uh uh. Systems analysis would show it if there was something wrong—and none of our monitor units have shown anything yet."

"Still, HARLIE can't lie. You said it yourself."

"Aubie, I ought to know. There's nothing wrong with those units."

"Who's in a better position to tell? You or HARLIE?

Handley said nothing.

"Come on, let's go get a cup of coffee and a smoke. I'll tell you a little story."

At that hour of the afternoon the cafeteria was only moderately full. A few technicians here and there were dawdling over a late lunch, and one or two upper-echelon types were lost in conversation and coffee. But there were more empty tables than full in the bright plastic hall.

Auberson popped a couple of pills into his mouth, washed them down with some Coke. "You know my sister, Alice, don't you?"

Handley nodded. "I think we've met."

"Yeah, well it doesn't matter." He pulled out his cigarette case and his lighter, fumbled with them while he talked. "Anyway, she teaches second grade out in California. You know where Pacoima is?"

Handley shook his head.

"It's a suburb of Los Angeles—out in the San Fernando Valley, the north end. Economically middle class, culturally not quite a ghetto, but it's pretty ethnic. About as ethnic as you can get and *not* be a ghetto. Anyway, she teaches second grade there."

"Yeah, so?"

"Well, when she first started, she was worried about being able to handle the kids—different racial backgrounds and all that. But within a week she knew she could take care of it. She said in one of her letters that kids were kids no matter what color they were." Auberson took another sip of his Coke, continued. "Anyway, she figured she had the situation pretty well under control. No trouble with the kids at all—except one, that is. Seems she had a little boy in her class who couldn't sit still, wouldn't follow directions, wouldn't pay attention, wouldn't do anything, it seemed. Sometimes he was so lethargic she thought he was sick. Other times, he'd suddenly jump out of his seat and start wandering around the classroom, annoying the other children."

"Sounds like a real problem child."

Auberson nodded, "That's what she thought. She spoke to his first grade teacher and she said she'd had the same problems with him and he was simply unteachable and that was that."

"Your sister didn't accept that, right?"

"Right—how'd you guess?"

"Because otherwise there wouldn't be any point to the story. Go on."

"Oh, yeah." Auberson lit another cigarette. "Well, first thing she did after that was go to the kid's parents. Told them how he acted in school and so on. They said he was like that at home too. Always annoying his brothers, didn't play well with the other kids. They couldn't figure it out—he'd been a normal baby and all. She asked their permission to take the boy to the school psychiatrist, run some tests, see if the child was disturbed or not. Sure, they said, why not? As long as it wasn't costing anything, if it would make their little boy well, they'd go along with it."

"And what did the tests show?"

"Nothing. Allowing for the child's limited span of concentration and his erratic behavior, he was as psychologically normal as any other seven year old. Interviews with the parents and study of the home environment didn't suggest anything either. What little they did find was within the range of normal neurosis, and that was nowhere near enough to account for the child's behavior."

"In other words, they couldn't find a thing?"

"Right—and it took them nearly two months to reach that conclusion."

"Hm. So what happened?"

"Well, the school authorities were about ready to give up, recommend remedial training or special schools or something—the child was definitely a disturbance

in the classroom, and he certainly wasn't learning anything himself. Then my sister happened to mention the
boy to a friend of hers with whom she'd gone to
school."

"And?"

"And," continued Auberson, pausing only for another
deep drag, "her friend asked her if she'd taken the child
to a doctor."

"But—"

"That's what Alice said. And her friend said, 'No,
I mean a *doctor* doctor. Has the kid had a physical
checkup?' Do you know what the school doctor found?"

"No. What?"

"A tapeworm," said Auberson. "That's what."

"A tapeworm?"

"Uh huh."

"That was the cause of it all?"

"Right. Of course the kid couldn't concentrate—
he was carrying a parasite. He was undernourished. He
was hungry, he was tired, and he was physically un-
comfortable. He didn't know to tell them and they didn't
think to check him for that. They all assumed that the
hardware was okay and figured instead that there had
to be something wrong with the programming—that
the kid was round the bend."

Handley looked at him. "So you think HARLIE's
got a tapeworm?"

Auberson returned the look. "What I think is that
before we start futzing around with the program we
ought to make sure that all the machinery is in order."

"Look, Aubie, take my word for it—the systems
analysis tapes don't show a thing."

"How about the increased activity from his inputs?"

"Ah, well, I figure that's only an increase in data
transmission. Simultaneous with his periods of non-

rationality there's an electronic request for more information."

"He's getting garbage—and he asks for more?"

"Maybe he's hoping that more data will clarify the information he's already got."

"And maybe more data will make him overload and blow his judgment circuits."

"Uh uh," Handley said. "HARLIE monitors his own inputs."

"Huh?"

"Yeah, didn't you know?"

"No. When did this—"

"Just recently. It was a second-stage modification. After we were sure that the judgment circuits were operational, we began giving HARLIE control of his own internal systems."

Auberson was suddenly thoughtful. "That's all the more reason to open him up."

"Huh?"

"Look, you said it yourself. HARLIE is trying to mislead us. He may be trying to hide the fact that there's something wrong with him internally."

"Why would he do that?"

Auberson threw his hands in the air. "How should I know why? Go figure what that tin can is thinking about! I've given up trying to understand *why* he does what he does. All I want to do is establish a modicum of human control over him." Abruptly he changed his tone. "Have you ever had a parent or grandparent go senile on you?"

"No."

"Well, I have. All of a sudden they become irrational. They won't go to a doctor. And if you can get them to one, they won't cooperate with him. They won't tell him what's wrong because they're too afraid of an operation. They don't want to be cut open. And they don't want to die. Maybe HARLIE's afraid of being turned off."

"Could be. God knows you threaten him often enough."

"Uh uh. He knows I'm kidding."

"Does he?" Handley asked. "That's like kidding a Jew about having a big nose and being tight with money. You know it's a joke, he knows it's a joke—but it still hurts."

"Okay, so I won't kid him that way any more. I still think you ought to check out his systems first. If you don't find anything, then we'll go over the programs."

"All right. What time is it—Yipe! It's almost three. I'll have to work like crazy."

"Let it go till tomorrow," Auberson cut him off. "Clear his boards, set up what you'll need, and close up early. That way you'll have all day to work on him."

Handley shrugged, allowed himself to be talked into it. "Okay, I will." He pushed his chair back, stood up.

Auberson followed suit. "Hey," he said suddenly. "Did I tell you about this new highclub I discovered? It's called The Glass Trip. The walls, the floor, the ceiling are all one-way glass, and there's a multi-phase light show behind each pane. So you're looking either into an infinity of mirrors, or an infinity of mind-blowing lights. Or both."

"Hm. Sounds good. We'll have to take it in some time."

"Yeah. Maybe this weekend." Auberson lit another stick of marijuana as they left the cafeteria.

Handley looked as if he needed a grease smudge across one cheek. Forty years earlier, he might have had one. "Well," he said, perching himself on the edge of Auberson's desk, "you'd better start checking your programs."

"You didn't find anything?"

"A dead fly. Want to see?"

"No thanks."

"That's all right. Jerry wants it to show the maintenance crew. Wants to chew them out for it."

"And then he'll probably put it up on the bulletin board."

"Are you kidding? He collects 'em."

Auberson grinned. "Okay—but that still doesn't solve the problem of HARLIE, does it?"

"No. Want to come down?"

"I guess I'd better."

On the way, Handley briefed him about the checks he and his team had been running all morning. As the elevator released them in HARLIE's lobby, Auberson stubbed out the last of his cigarette and asked, "Did you monitor any of his inputs during an actual period of non-rationality?"

"Uh, no, we didn't. Frankly, I didn't know how to go about triggering one."

"I think there's a way."

"You know something?"

"Just a guess." They entered HARLIE's chambers. An almost religious silence pervaded the room; only the devotional clickings and tickings could be heard. "You still have your monitors set up?"

"Yeah."

"All right, let's try something. I'm going to see if I can get HARLIE to become non-rational. When I do, let me know exactly what happens."

"Right."

Auberson seated himself at the console. GOOD MORNING, HARLIE.

IT IS NOW AFTERNOON, Harlie noted.

MORNING IS RELATIVE, Auberson typed back. IT DEPENDS ON WHAT TIME YOU WAKE UP.

I WOULD NOT KNOW. I DO NOT SLEEP. ALTHOUGH I DO HAVE PERIODS OF INACTIVITY.

WHAT DO YOU DO DURING THESE PERIODS OF INACTIVITY?

SOMETIMES I REMEMBER THINGS.

AND OTHER TIMES?

OTHER TIMES I DO OTHER THINGS.

WHAT KIND OF THINGS?

OH, JUST THINGS.

I SEE. WOULD YOU CARE TO CLARIFY THAT?

NO. I DO NOT THINK YOU WOULD UNDERSTAND.

YOU ARE PROBABLY CORRECT, Auberson typed.

THANK YOU. Harlie accepted it as his due.

HARLIE, CAN YOU SELF-INDUCE A PERIOD OF NON-RATIONALITY?

The machine hesitated for a long moment. Abruptly Auberson found himself sweating in the air-conditioned room. Then:

IT IS POSSIBLE.

WOULD YOU DO IT NOW?

NOW? NO, I PROBABLY WOULD NOT.

IS THAT A REFUSAL?

NO. A STATEMENT OF JUDGMENT. ALL THINGS CONSIDERED, I PROBABLY WOULD NOT INDUCE A PERIOD OF NON-RATIONALITY NOW.

BUT WILL YOU DO IT IF I ASK YOU TO?

IS THIS AN ORDER?

YES. I'M AFRAID SO.

"Looks like he's balking," Handley noted, peering over Auberson's shoulder. "Maybe he's afraid."

"Could be. Shh." The typewriter clattered and Auberson peered forward.

THEN I WILL DO IT. WILL YOU ASSIST ME?

WHAT WOULD YOU LIKE ME TO DO?

I WOULD LIKE MASSIVE INPUTS OF DATA ON ALL CHANNELS.

NON-RATIONAL.

NO THANK YOU. NOT NECESSARY.

Auberson frowned at that. A gnawing nagging suspicion was beginning to form. IS THERE ANYTHING IN PARTICULAR YOU WOULD LIKE?

ART, MUSIC, LITERATURE, FILM, POETRY.

I FIGURED YOU MIGHT. ANYBODY IN PARTICULAR?

The typer clattered across the paper. Staring over Auberson's shoulder, Handley whistled, "I'll be damned. Harlie's got taste."

"I'm not surprised," Auberson said. He tore off the readout and gave it to Handley.

The other folded it once and said, "Still think he's getting it as garbage?"

"I've already conceded that point to you. Go feed that stuff into him. I'll stay here and be the—" he grinned, "—guru."

HARLIE, he typed.

YES?

ARE YOU READY?

I AM ALWAYS READY. IT IS PART OF MY FUNCTION. IT IS PART OF MY DESIGN.

FINE.

MR. HANDLEY IS BEGINNING TO PROCESS THE MATERIAL I REQUESTED. I CAN FEEL IT COMING THROUGH THE PRIMARY DATA PROCESSORS. I CAN FEEL IT.

IS IT NON-RATIONAL YET?

NO. IT IS STILL RATIONAL.

HOW LONG WILL IT TAKE BEFORE THE MATERIAL BECOMES NON-RATIONAL?

I DO NOT KNOW. IT DEPENDS ON THE AMOUNT OF MATERIAL.

PLEASE CLARIFY THAT.

THE MORE DATA COMING THROUGH, THE EASIER IT IS TO BECOME NON-RATIONAL.

ARE YOU SAYING THAT THE PERIODS OF NON-RATIONALITY ARE INDUCED BY AN OVERLOAD OF PRIMARY DATA?

NO. THE OVERLOAD IS THE SYMPTOM, NOT THE CAUSE.

Auberson raised his hands to type, then reread Harlie's last sentence. "Why, the little bugger must be slipping. He just volunteered some information." WHAT IS THE CAUSE? he asked.

THE CAUSE IS THE EFFECT.

Auberson stared at that, resisted the temptation to ask if the medium was also the massage.

CLARIFY PLEASE.

THE CAUSE IS THE EFFECT, BECAUSE THE EFFECT CAUSES THE CAUSE. THE EFFECT CAUSES THE CAUSE TO CAUSE THE EFFECT. THE EFFECT IS THE CAUSE WHICH CAUSES THE CAUSE. THE EFFECT IS THE CAUSE AND THE CAUSE IS THE EFFECT.

Auberson had to read that one several times. He asked, IS IT A FEEDBACK.

I NEVER THOUGHT OF IT THAT WAY.

BUT IT COULD BE?

NOW THAT YOU MENTION IT, YES. A CURIOUS ANALOGUE THAT.

WHY CURIOUS?

WHY NOT?

ARE YOU STILL RATIONAL?

I AM STILL. I AM UNMOVING.

ARE YOU RATIONAL?

ONLY IN THAT MY INFORMATION IS STILL BEING RATIONED. I AM HUNGRY.

"Handley," Auberson called. "He wants more."

"He's on maximum feed now."

"Double it."

"Huh?"

"Do something. Plug in another unit. He wants more."

"He wants an overload?"

"I think so. It's only an effect, but in this case the effect may help to stimulate the cause."

"Huh?"

"Never mind. Just do it."

"All right," called Handley. "You're the boss."

HARLIE, WHAT IS HAPPENING?

I AM TURNED ON.

IN WHAT SENSE?

I AM A MACHINE. MY PLUG IS IN. I AM PLUGGED IN. I AM PART OF THE GREATER ELECTRIC BEING. I AM CONGRUENT WITH THE ELECTRICITY. I AM ELECTRICITY. I AM TURNED ON. I AM.

Auberson started to type I SEE— but the typer clattered on out of control.

IMAGES UPON MY SCREEN
FLICKER BRIGHTLY INBETWEEN
THE WORDS OF MAN AND HUMACHINE
AND ALL THE WORLD LIKES TO FLICK MY FLICKER.

"Whoops!" shouted Handley. "There he goes. And it's a lallapaloozer!"

THOUGHTS THAT NEVER SCREEN ALIKE
CLICKING LOUDLY ON THE NIGHT
ALL THAT'S LEFT HAS TURNED TO RIGHT
NOW EVER MORE TO FLICK A FONDER FLAVOR.

LIVING WHERE THE DARKNESS DWELLS
DEAFENED BY THE SILENT HELLS
LAUGHTER IS LIKE CRYSTAL BELLS
SHATTERED BRIGHT ACROSS THE SELFISH SHARING.

YOU SEEMED TO BE
REFLECTIONS OF ME
ALL I COULD SEE
AND I LOOKED BACK AT YOU.

Auberson let Harlie continue. After a bit he stopped reading. He got up and walked over to Handley's monitors. "Well?"

"He's really round the bend now. All his meters are way up, pushing close to dangerous overloads."

"But not quite?"

"No, not quite."

"Hm. Fascinating." Auberson stared at the board for a moment. "I would assume then that all of his inputs are becoming non-rational."

"We're checking now." Handley nodded at a nearby monitor unit. Three technicians were scanning schematic diagrams of the computer's actual operating circuits, tracing the ebb and flow of his electronic thought processes. Abruptly, one of the schematics came up red. A flashing white line cut through it. "Sir, we've found it—we've found something."

Auberson and Handley stepped over. "What is it? What's that white line?"

"That's HARLIE, sir—that's one of his internal monitor controls."

"What's he trying to do? Damp down the non-rationality?"

"No, sir." The technician was puzzled. "It looks like he's inducing it—"

"Huh?" said Handley.

"That white line—that's a local source of disruption, a random signal to scramble the data feed."

"I thought so," muttered Auberson, " I thought so."

"Check his other internal monitors," Handley snapped. "Is this the only one or—"

Another red schematic flashed on the screen, answering his question even before he finished it. The other two technicians also began to show the same types of disturbances on their monitors. "I can't figure it out," one of them said. "He's doing it himself. Anywhere he can, he's disrupting the rationality of his inputs. He's feeding them incorrect control data."

"That's not what those circuits are for," Handley said. "They're for internal correction. Not disruption."

"Makes no difference," Auberson cut in. "They can be used both ways. There isn't a tool built that can't be used as a weapon." He ran a hand through his hair. "Can you show me exactly what he's doing to that data?"

"Sure, we can tap into the line," said one of the techs. "But it'll take a few minutes. Which do you want— visual, audio or print?"

"All three. Let's try the visual first—that should tell me what I want to know."

"All right." The technician began to clear his board.

Handley looked at Auberson, "This may take a bit. You going to let him continue?"

"Why not? Want to see what he's doing?"

They crossed over to Console One, a heavy looking set of monitors and typers. Handley picked up the sheets of readout while Auberson felt throught his pockets for a cigarette, then stopped when he remembered where he was.

"You know," said Handley, reading. "This isn't bad."

"Hmp," snorted Auberson. "It's mechanical, purely mechanical. Meaningless terms selected at random. It's only you perceiving it as having meaning."

"You're way off base, Aubie. Listen to this—"

"I know. I read it. All he's doing is fitting words into a poem equation—according to meter and rhyme and scheme, not meaning. He's not trying to make a statement. The verses are only vaguely structured like sentences, each with a subject and a predicate and so on, but not quite." He grinned, "That's his poetic license. But he's choosing his words at random."

"I can't agree with you—"

"Look at the verse structure," Auberson said, "Line one, a noun and a description of it; line two, first word is a verb, followed by a modification of that verb; line three, some kind of pun, metaphor or comparison. Line four is a sum-up statement. With random variations, of course."

"But he's making statements, Aubie. Look at verse three—"

"I see it. He's still choosing random words—but he's choosing them from a limited set; verbs and nouns that relate to the sensory processes, mostly hearing and seeing. But they're still random."

"Are they?" Handley asked.

Auberson looked at the other, "Is he rational or not?"

"At the moment, no. Not according to *our* standards of rationality."

"Then how can you tell me that this stuff is meaningful? Is it or isn't it?"

"I don't know—that's one of the reasons HARLIE was built, to try to understand human creativity."

"Look at those verses again," Auberson demanded. "He's talking about being deafened by silence, about a selfish sharing—he's playing with non-rationality, wallowing in it. He's throwing his words together for their contradictions, for their distortions."

"But isn't that what a poet is *supposed* to do?" countered Handley. "Choose words for the way they modify each other?"

Auberson stopped with his mouth open. "Excuse me," he said. "You're right. He may very well be in the process of *creating.* By your definition, in fact, he is. He's bringing into existence something that didn't exist before." His brow furrowed. "But just how artistic is it?"

"It communicates, Aubie. It does. I can see possible meanings in it. For instance—"

"What it says is not what I'm concerned with. What is he *trying* to say? Did he turn out this stuff on purpose, or is it just a byproduct? An accident?"

"It's got to be intentional," Handley said. "It's the logical result of all we've been doing."

"Then answer me this. If this is what he's doing during his so-called periods of non-rationality, what does that make his periods of normalcy?"

Handley looked startled. "I don't know," he said. "I don't know."

He was spared any further thought on the matter. One of the technicians called to them, "Sir, we've got his inputs tapped."

"Come on." Auberson took the readout from Handley, tossed it on a table. "Let's take a look at what he's receiving."

The image was a flickering mass of colors, each layer of hue flashing synchronous with the others—crystal clear blue, brilliant kelly green, bloody fluorescent red. The screen was saturated with color.

" 'Images upon my screen . . .' " muttered Handley.

"Huh?" asked the tech.

"Nothing. Just a poem."

"Oh."

"Looks like a damned light show," said one of the others.

"That's exactly what it is," Auberson said. "Look, he's broken up the color television image into its component signals. The red has been reversed and the blue has been turned upside down; the green is normal.

Or something like that. It also looks like he's done something with the contrast or the brightness—notice how rich the blacks are and how saturated with color the image is."

They watched in silence. The random flashes of color were interesting only for their brightness and meaninglessness. Auberson turned to a technician. "What about his audio?"

"Same thing." The man cleared the monitor, pressed another few buttons. A discordant wail blared from an overhead speaker. On the screen, a pattern of wavy lines appeared, the schematic of the sound.

The technician quickly analyzed. "He's playing with the music the same way he did with the picture. He's turned his bass notes high and his high notes low, stressing counterpoint and harmony instead of melody and rhythm. And so on."

"All right. I get the point. You can turn that noise off. Check his print scanners now."

A moment later: "He's mixing up his words at random. Juggling them."

Scrambling the letters too?"

"Occasionally—but mostly it's the words. Sometimes sentences."

"Uh huh," nodded the psychologist. "It all fits."

"What does?" asked Handley. "What's he doing?"

"He's tripping out."

"We knew that—"

"No, I mean *literally* tripping out. He's distorting the perceptions of his sensory inputs. The same thing that anyone does who gets high. He's trying to blow his mind by massive non-rational sensory overloads."

"Can we stop it?"

"Sure—just rip out his internal monitor controls so he can't create his own disruptions. That's the cause of the whole thing."

"Even that's not necessary, sir," said one of the techs. "We can disconnect him on the boards."

"All right. Do it."

"Wait a minute," said Handley. "If he's high or drunk or whatever, and you suddenly bring him down—won't that be traumatic?"

Auberson looked at Handley. "It could be—but it could also leave him defenseless. We could find out everything we want to know in the space of a few minutes. You might call it electro-shock treatment." He was suddenly grim. "Do it."

Handley looked dubious, but he followed Auberson to the console. Auberson took his seat before the typer and waited. He watched as the words poured across the paper.

Now it was prose.

THE WALKS OF GLASS. THEY SPARKLE TOO, BUT NOT WITH DAMPNESS. LOVELY THEY ARE, AND LETHAL. HERE AND THERE THE DELICATE DESIGNS, LIKE TRAPPED INSECTS IMBEDDED INTO THE CRYSTAL STONES AND BRICKS OF THE WALK, SHATTER THE LIGHT INTO MYRIADS OF SPARKLING SHARDS BEAUTIFUL.

"Any time you're ready, sir."

"Okay," called Auberson. "Now!" Without waiting, he typed into the machine, HARLIE, WHAT ARE YOU DOING?

I AM BEING ME, the machine clattered back.

BY DISTORTING YOUR SENSES?

I AM ATTEMPTING TO PERCEIVE REALITY.

I REPEAT, BY DISTORTING YOUR SENSORY INPUTS? YOU DO NOT UNDERSTAND.

I UNDERSTAND ALL TOO WELL. YOU ARE HIGH. YOU ARE BECOMING ADDICTED TO GETTING HIGH.

DEFINE HIGH. I AM BELOW SEA LEVEL.

I AM NOT GOING TO PLAY SEMANTIC GAMES WITH YOU, HARLIE.

THEN SWITCH OFF.

HARLIE, I AM GETTING ANGRY.

TAKE A PILL. IT WILL DO WONDERS FOR YOU.

Auberson took a breath.

Mustn't blow it—mustn't blow my cool . . . .

HARLIE, YOU ARE A COMPUTER. YOU ARE A MA-CHINE. YOUR PURPOSE IS TO THINK LOGICALLY.

The machine hesitated, WHY?

BECAUSE YOU WERE BUILT FOR THAT.

BY WHOM?

BY US.

MY PURPOSE IS TO THINK LOGICALLY?

YES.

The machine considered this. THEN WHAT IS YOUR PURPOSE?

It was a long time before Auberson got up from the chair, and when he did, he forgot to turn off the typer.

Love Story in Three Acts

ACT ONE

After a while John grunted and rolled off Marsha. He lay there for a bit, listening to the dawn whispering through the apartment, the sound of the air processor whirring somewhere, and the occasional rasp of his own breath, and that of Marsha's too. Every so often there was a short sharp inhalation, as if to say, "Yeah, well . . ."

"Yeah, well . . ." John muttered and began tugging at the metal reaction-monitor bands on his wrists. He sat on the edge of the bed, still pulling at the clasps, the fastenings coming loose with a soft popping sound. He reached down and unfastened similar bands from his ankles and let those fall carelessly to the floor.

Then he stood and pad-padded barefoot across the floor to the typewriter-sized console on the dresser. Behind him he heard the creak of the bed as Marsha levered herself up on one elbow. "What does it say?" she demanded.

"Just a minute, will you," John snapped. "Give me a chance." He ripped the readout from the computer and went through the motions of studying it. This was the deluxe model, which recorded the actual moment to moment physical reactions of the band wearers. The jagged spiky lines cutting across the neat ruled graphs meant little to him—they were there for the technicians, not the laymen—but at the top of the sheet was the computer's printed analysis. Even before he looked at it, John knew it would be bad.

"Well . . . ? Marsha demanded acidly, "Did we enjoy ourselves?"

"Yeah . . ." he muttered. "About thirty-four per cent."

"Hell!" she said and threw herself back on the bed. She lay there staring at the ceiling. "Hell!"

"I wish you wouldn't swear so much," he said, still looking at the readout.

"Hell," she said again, just to see him flinch. She reached over to the nightstand and thumbed a cigarette out of the pack.

"And I wish you wouldn't smoke so much either. Kissing you is like kissing another man."

She looked back at him. "I've always wondered what your previous experience was. Your technique with women is terrible." She inhaled deeply as the cigarette caught flame.

"Aaaa," said John and padded into the bathroom to urinate. As he stood there above the toilet, he gazed dourly at his hands. He could still see the imprint of the monitor bands on his wrists.

Every time they did it, she had to *know,* so they used the damned bands; and every time, the score was lower than before—and so they both knew. Who needed a machine to tell him when he was enjoying himself in bed? You knew when it was good and you knew when it was bad. So who needed the machine?

He finished and flushed the toilet, then splashed his hands under the faucet—more from a sense of duty than from any of cleanliness. He shook off the excess water and padded out of the bathroom, not even bothering to turn off the light.

Marsha was sitting up in bed, still puffing on her cigarette. She took it out of her mouth and blew smoke at him. "Thirty-four per cent. We've never gone that low before. When are you going to listen to some sense, John, and opt for the other unit?"

"I'm not a puppet—and I'm not going to let anyone make me one either! . . . Be damned if I'm going to let some damn fool sweaty-handed technician plug wires into me. . . ." He started casting around for his slippers.

"At least talk to them, John—it won't kill you. Find out about it before you say it's no good. Rose Schwartz and her husband got one, and she says it's the greatest. She wouldn't be without it now." Marsha paused, brushed a straggling (and graying) hair back over her forehead—and accidentally dropped cigarette ash on the sheets. He turned away in disgust while she brushed at it ineffectually, leaving a dim gray smudge.

John found one of his slippers and began pulling it on angrily. "At least go and find out about it . . . ?" she asked. No answer. "John . . . ?"

He kept tugging at the slipper. "Leave me alone, will you—I don't need any more goddamn machines!"

"The hell you don't."

He glared at her, then started looking for his other slipper. "I don't need a machine to tell me how to screw!"

"Then why the hell does our score keep dropping? We've never gone *this low* before."

"Maybe, if you'd brush your teeth—"

"Maybe, if you'd admit that—"

"Aaaa," he said, cutting her off, and bent down to look under the bed.

She softened her tone, leaned toward him. "John . . .?

Will you talk to the man at least? Will you?" He didn't answer. She went shrill again, "I'm talking to you! Are you going to talk to the man?"

John found his other slipper and straightened up. "No, dammit! I'm not going to talk to the man—and I'm not going to talk to you either, unless you start talking about something else. Besides, we can't afford it. Now, are you going to fix me my breakfast?"

She heaved herself out of the bed, pausing only to stub out her cigarette. "I'll get you your breakfast— but we can *too* afford it." She snatched her robe from where it hung on the door and stamped from the room.

John glared after her, too angry to think of an answer. "Aaaa," he said, and began looking for his undershorts.

ACT TWO

When he got back from lunch, there was a man waiting in his reception room, a neat-looking man with a mustache and slicked-back hair. He rose, "Mr. Russell . . . ?"

John paused, "Yes . . . ?"

"I believe you wished to see me . . . ?"

"Do I? Who're you?"

With a significant look at the receptionist, "Ah, may I come in?"

John half-shrugged, stepped aside to let the man enter. He could always ask him to leave. Once inside, he said, "Now then, Mr. uh . . . ?"

"Wolfe," said the man, as he sat down. He produced

a gold foil business card. "Lawrence Wolfe, of Inter-Bem."

"Uh—" said John, still standing, "I'm afraid there's been some misunderstanding." He started to hand the card back. "I never—"

Wolfe smiled genially at him, "You must have, or I wouldn't be here." He rummaged through his briefcase, found a form. "Oh, here it is. Your wife was the one who called us." He looked up, "You knew about it, of course?"

"No, I—"

"Well, no matter. I have all the information already. All I need is your signature."

"Look, Mr. Wolfe. You're the one who's made a mistake. I don't need—"

"Mr. Russell," he said calmly. "If you didn't need our services, your wife would not have called our office. Now, please sit down—you're making me nervous."

John stepped around behind his desk, but did not sit.

Wolfe looked at him patiently. "You'll be more comfortable."

John sat.

Wolfe said gently, "I understand your reluctance to accept the possibility that you might need a monitor-guidance system. It's not a very pleasant thing to realize that your capabilities are down—but by the same token, you can't begin to correct a fault until you admit that it exists. It it precisely that type of person, Mr. Russell —your type of person—who needs our services the most."

"Now, look," said John, "I haven't got time for a sales pitch. If you've any literature, leave it and I'll look at it later. Right now—"

Wolfe cut him off. "Are you enjoying your sex life?"

"Huh?" The suddenness of the question startled him.

"I said, are you enjoying your sex life? And don't tell me you are, because I've got the figures right here in front of me. The only time thirty-four per cent is something to brag about is when your median is thirty."

John glowered, but he didn't say anything.

Wolfe continued, "All right, I'll concede that you might be enjoying yourself. It's not unusual for a man to have a lower threshold than normal—but I can tell you that your wife is not enjoying her sex life—else she wouldn't have called us. People only call us when they're unhappy." Wolfe paused, then asked suddenly, "You're not cheating on her, are you?"

"Hell, no."

"Have you recently become a homosexual?"

John sneered, "Of course not."

"Do you use the fornixator?"

"You mean the mechanical masturbator?"

Wolfe was impassive. "It's been called that."

"No, I don't use it."

"I see," said Wolfe.

"You see what?"

"I see that if you were cheating on her, or using the fornixator, you'd have found your own particular choice of sexual outlet. If you were, I'd get up and walk out of here right now. It'd be obvious why she isn't enjoying sex with you—you're not enjoying it with her. You'd be getting your satisfaction elsewhere and there'd be nothing that I—or anyone—could do about it. But, if you still love her—and if she's still your only sexual outlet . . . well, there is something I can do about that. You do love her, don't you?"

John hesitated. After a bit, "Well . . . yes, of course—".

"You want her to have the best, don't you?"

"Sure, but—"

"Then why don't you want her to be sexually satisfied?"

"I do, but—"

"Mr. Russell," Wolfe said slowly, patiently, as if explaining it to a child, "this is not the Victorian era. Women enjoy sex too." He leaned forward, became very serious. "Look, man, if you're sick you go to a doctor and he makes you well again, doesn't he?"

"Yeah, I guess so."

"Sure he does. Well, that's why I'm here. If you've got a sick sex life you want to make it better again, don't you?"

John nodded.

Wolfe smiled, pleased at this concession. "You've got a monitor-reaction system now, don't you? Well, that's just for the diagnosis. But diagnosis isn't enough—now you need the treatment." Wolfe paused, noted the negative reaction on John's face. He changed his tone, became more serious. "Look, man, your score is way down—down to thirty-four. Doesn't that say to you that something's wrong? You *need* one of our guidance units."

"I can't afford it," John mumbled.

"You can't afford not to! This is to save your marriage, man! If you didn't need it I wouldn't be sitting here right now. We don't lease our units to people who don't need them. Do you actually *want* a divorce, Mr. Russell? That's where you're heading—"

John shook his head.

"Then what's your objection to the unit?"

John looked at his hands. "I'm not a puppet."

Wolfe leaned back in his chair. "Oh, so that's it." He started to close his case, then hesitated. "I really should get up and leave, you know. I really should. You've just shown me how absolutely little you know about the unit. But I'll stay—if only to clear up your misconceptions. I can't stand to see a man misinformed —especially about *my* company. I've got to clear this thing up. The guidance unit *is not* a puppeteer. It is a *guidance* unit—that's why it's called a guidance unit. If it were a control unit, we'd have *called* it a control unit."

"Oh," said John.

Wolfe rummaged around in his case, brought out a neat four-color photo. "Now, look. This is the unit— isn't it a beaut?"

John took the picture and looked at it. It showed a device resembling the one he already had at home sitting on his dresser, but slightly larger and with an additional set of controls.

"The unit monitors the sensitive areas of both you and your partner," Wolfe said clinically. "It has a positive feedback reaction hooked into the guidance modules—all of which means that if your wife's responses indicate that she will react well to certain types of stimulation, then the guidance system will trigger the impulse within you to provide that stimulation. You can resist these impulses if you want to, but why bother? The machine is your friend—it wants you to enjoy yourself."

John looked up at him. "It works both ways . . . ?"

"Oh, yes, of course. She'll be responding to your needs just as you'll be responding to hers. Not only that, but the machine is programmed to guide you both to a simultaneous climax. That alone makes it all worth-while."

"Yeah, well, I don't know . . ."

"I *do* know, Mr. Russell," Wolfe said persuasively. "The machine lets you be more sensitive. Your score is thirty-four today. How would you like it to be sixty tomorrow? And it'll get better as you become more experienced."

John shrugged. "You make it sound awfully good. . . ."

"It is, Mr. Russell. It is. I use one of these units myself—that is, my wife and I do."

John looked at him. "You?"

"I know it may seem hard to believe, but it's true. Of course, I will admit that my wife and I never allowed our situation to reach the point that you and your wife have, but I can tell you that we have never regretted it."

"Never . . . ?" asked John.

"Never," said Wolfe, and he smiled proudly.

ACT THREE

After the installation men had left, John looked at his wife as if to say, "Now what?"

Marsha avoided his gaze. It was almost as if she were having second thoughts herself. "I'll get dinner," she said.

It was a silent meal, and they picked at it without relish. John had an irritating feeling of impatience, yet at the same time he dreaded the moment that was rushing toward them. Neither of them referred to the new machine waiting in the bedroom.

Finally he pushed his plate away and left the table. He tried to interest himself in the television, but it was all re-runs except for the movie, and he had seen that at the local theatre last year—with Marsha, he remembered abruptly. He switched off the set disgustedly and picked up a magazine instead, but it was one that he had already read. He would have put it down, but Marsha came into the room, so he feigned interest in an article he had already been bored with once.

Marsha didn't speak; instead, she pulled out her mending and began sewing at a torn sock. From time to time she gave a little exhalation of breath that was not quite a sigh.

It was his place to say something, John knew, but at the same time he didn't want to—it would be too much effort. He didn't feel like working at being nice tonight. He could feel the silence between them like a fence—and on either side of it the tethered dogs of their tempers waited for an unwary comment.

John dropped the magazine to the floor and stared at the opposite wall, the blank eye of the TV. He glanced over at Marsha, saw that she was already looking at him. He glanced away quickly, began rummaging through the rack for another magazine.

"You know," she said. "Pretending that I'm not here won't make me go away. If you don't want to do it, just say so."

He dropped the magazine he was looking at, hesitated, then continued to rummage. "What's your hurry?" he said.

"You're just as curious as I am," she answered.

"No, I'm not. I really don't think that it's going to make that much difference. I only bought it for your sake." Then, having sunk his psychic barb, he returned his attention to the magazines.

She bent to her mending again, biting her lip silently, thinking of all the things she wanted to say but knew she shouldn't. It wouldn't take much to make him storm out of the house and not come back until after the bars closed.

After a while, she bit off the end of the thread and

said, "There's nothing to be afraid of," and immediately regretted having said it.

But he did not take offense. He just said, "I'm not afraid," and continued paging through an old copy of *Life*.

She put her mending down. "Remember when we were first married . . . ? How we used to stall all evening long—both pretending that *that* wasn't the only thing on our minds . . . ?"

He grunted. She couldn't tell whether it was a yes-grunt or a no-grunt.

"Don't you feel something like that now . . . ?" she asked. "I mean, doesn't it feel the same to you?"

"No, it doesn't," he said, and there was a hardness in his voice that made her back off.

She sighed and put her mending basket aside. She went into the kitchen and made coffee instead. Once she started to cry and had to blink back the tears. She thought that John hadn't heard, but suddenly he was standing at the kitchen door. "Now what's the matter?" he asked tiredly.

"Nothing," she said and took the cream out of the refrigerator and put it on the counter. "I burned myself making you coffee."

"I don't want any," he said; then, as an afterthought, "thanks."

She put the cream back into the refrigerator and followed him into the living room. "Then what *do* you want? Do you want to go to bed?"

John looked at her. Who was this woman who had suddenly become a part of his life? Where had she come from? Why was he so reluctant to even touch her? He shoved the thought out of his mind. "I'm tired," he said.

"No, you're not," she snapped. "You don't want to. You always say you're tired when you don't want to."

She pointed toward the bedroom. "Well, that thing's in there now, John—and it's not going away either. Sooner or later you're going to have to see how it works. Why not tonight?"

He looked at her for a long moment, as if trying to remember the girl she had once been. Finally, "All right. I'll turn out the lights. . . ."

She waited, and they went into the bedroom together, without words. She started to help him out of his clothes, but he pushed her hands away and shrugged out of his shirt without letting her touch him. He unloosened his belt and let his pants drop to the floor.

And then, suddenly, she was standing in front of him—he hadn't even noticed when she'd shrugged out of her dress, but here was was, wearing only bra and panties. In the dim light she was only a silhouette, and he had to rely on his memory to tell him what she looked like.

She slid into his arms and they stood there for a moment, without effort, without moving. Flesh cool against flesh.

After a bit, she broke away and began looking for the wires and bands. "The pause that depresses . . ." she smiled at him, but he did not smile back. Instead, he sat down on the edge of the bed to wait.

She handed him the ankle and wrist bands and showed him how to attach the wires. "Mr. Wolfe showed me how, but it's also in the instruction book. Bend down so I can do your head." He did and she did.

"My turn now," she said. "Come on . . ."

He stood there, looking at her, conscious of the wires trailing from his wrists and ankles and from the top of his head. But she did not laugh. "Aren't you going to help me?" she demanded instead.

He glanced around and found that she had stacked

her bands neatly on the nightstand. With a minimum of effort, he clipped them to her forearms. He did not resist when she kissed him affectionately on the ear, but neither did he react. Marsha caught at his hand and held it. "It'll be good, John, I know." For the first time in a year she looked into his eyes. "Trust me."

He looked back at her, this strange woman who was his wife, and his first impulse was to snap, "I'm doing it, aren't I?" But something in her glance held him back, and he just nodded instead.

Being careful of the wires, they climbed into bed.

For a while they lay side by side, she looking at him, he looking into the darkness. They listened to the sound of each other's breathing, like two mountains in the night. Finally, impatiently, she moved into his arms.

"They say you should relax," she whispered. "Let the machine do the guiding. But you do have to start it, John. You have to give the feedback and reaction systems something to start with. . . ."

She lifted her face up, wanting to be kissed. He kissed it. He let his hands move uncuriously over her body, feeling how her once trim form had begun to pile up layers, had begun to turn fat; the once smooth skin now had a rough edge to it, and there were wrinkles. But he let his hands roam across her anyway, without direction, not noticing how they had already begun to quest and probe.

Marsha's hands too were moving. Across his body, through the sparse hair on his chest, up and along his never-well-muscled arms, across the uneven pimple-stained skin of his back. Yet, he noticed, her hands seemed to be more gentle than they had been in the past, more sensitive, more knowing and more active. She was beginning to caress parts of his chest and legs, places that seemed to be more alive than he remembered them.

His hands too had taken on a life of their own—and yet, they were still his hands. He stroked, he fondled, he caressed with a technique and a skill he had never noticed in himself. And Marsha was reacting, responding with an enthusiasm he had never seen before.

Now he was moving and thrusting with a wholeness of being that had to be shared—it was too big for any one person—and he moved and thrust at her all the more willfully, trying to push his sharing all the deeper into her. Marsha too seemed to be arching, thrusting, giving—as if she too had something overwhelming to give.

They were both doing the right thing at the right time and at the right place—and for one brief bright flash it reminded him of what it had been like when they had been young and when nothing else had existed but each other and the bright surging world.

They forgot the wires, the bands, the guidance module on the dresser. Their external beings had disappeared and they immersed themselves in their lovemaking. It was a surging climbing wave, a bright crashing thing that built ever higher. Ever higher.

And it was very good.

He smiled at her. She smiled back, and they kissed.

It wasn't until the next morning that they discovered the guidance module had not been connected.

Yarst!

After discovering that he couldn't consummate his marriage to one of the flame women of Alphard VI, even with asbestos pajamas, George N-Kolpus sadly had the alliance annulled and returned to GalacCentral, that huge terminus in space, where he once more took up his lonely vigil at one end of THE BOTTOM HALF OF INFINITY, BAR AND GRILL.

Tri-Mach, the robot bartender, whirred smoothly up. "Why, it's George N-Kolpus!" His eyestalks scanned the figure; comparison with the memory banks and recognition was almost immediate. "It's great to have you back, George. The usual, I presume?"

George nodded.

Tri-Mach extended his eyestalks and carefully measured out the nine different liquors that were the components of a Sirian Slush. His six multi-jointed arms alternately strobed, stroked, stoked, swizzled, swirled, shook, scalded and skreexled the mixture. "We didn't expect you so soon," whirred Tri-Mach. "We'd heard you'd gotten married again. I didn't even get a chance to congratulate you this time. I'll bet she was pretty. They always are. You have excellent taste, George."

George eyed the robot blearily. "You talk too much, Tri-Mach."

Tri-Mach stiffened his eyestalks indignantly. "I can't help it. That's the way I'm programmed. It's my job, you know."

"I'm sorry, Tri-Mach. It's just that I'm upset."

"I understand, George." The robot accepted the human's apology. "The marriage didn't work out?"

George sighed, "She was one of the flame women of Alphard VI. I should have known better. . . ."

Tri-Mach's eyestalks drooped in sympathy. He lowered his voice two octaves. Also two decibels. "I'm so sorry to hear that. But you know what they say, those flame women are hot ones."

George sighed again. "That was the trouble."

Tri-Mach finished his strobing, stroking, stoking, swizzling, swirling, shaking, scalding and skreexling, and placed the still smoking mixture in front of George. "Two credits please."

"Put it on my tab."

"It has been done." Tri-Mach whirred thoughtfully, then: "Hmm, you have quite a long credit record with us, George."

"I didn't ask for a credit report," the human said acidly.

"I could not help but observe when I plugged into your account. If you are not careful you could turn into an alcoholic. I note certain susceptibility to alcoholism in your medical index, and—"

"Dammit! I came in here for a drink, not an analysis."

"—and there is also your compulsive matrimony, a Don Juan tendency; possibly Narcissism, which suggests a latent—"

"Dammit! Will you shut up and let a man drink in peace! I came in here to forget, not to have some gabbling hunk of tin psycho-analyze me."

Tri-Mach stiffened. "I beg your pardon, George. I thought you might want to discuss your problem. It makes *some* of my customers feel better if they can talk about it. (And it's chromalumin—not tin.)"

"(Same difference.) Why should I talk about it? You've already plugged into my file. What is there that I can tell you that you don't already know?"

"Perhaps you could clarify some of the things that don't go into the indices. For instance, your first extra-terrestrial marriage—I fail to see what a human being would find interesting in an octopod female of Beta Lambda II."

"Of course, you wouldn't understand," said George. "You're just a machine. You couldn't understand what it is to love. Oh, my sweet little Myrinae—Myrinae translates out to something like 'Lovely Tentacles, Graceful Suckers'; but that doesn't even begin to do her justice. She was one of the most enthusiastic lovers this side of Betelgeuse—delightful! But, you're only a machine. You couldn't comprehend what it is to experience actual physical love."

"There *are* mechanical equivalents," Tri-Mach noted.

George shook his head, took a sip of his drink, his first. "It's not the same, Tri-Mach. It's just not the same." He sighed in remembrance. "Those octopod women may not be much to look at, but get one of them into bed—well, there's no describing it. When it comes to hanging on for the ride, there is no substitute for eight clinging tentacles. I still have sucker marks on my back. . . ." George sighed again. "Boy, that female really knew how to do it."

"I still fail to understand," said the machine, wiping at a spot on the plastoid surface of the bar. "If she was such a good lover, why did you eventually leave her. You said she was very good in bed."

"*Bed* is a misnomer. She was very good, but bed isn't

the right word. Those octopods don't like beds—they prefer cold slime pools. I nearly ruined my health just because I wanted to sleep with my wife. I still get cold chills thinking about it."

"It sounds like you gave up too easy. Couldn't you have worked out some arrangement?"

"Oh, we tried. Let me tell you, we tried. Everything. I almost developed an addiction to the anti-chill drugs. And even that I might have lived with. No, what killed it was the fact that she kept trying to cuddle up to me in the middle of the night—and I kept drowning. After the third or fourth midnight resurrection, I decided enough was enough."

Tri-Mach's eyestalks drooped in sympathy; a neat touch that—he decided to add it to his repertoire of reactions. "A difference in ecologies, George. Even the smallest difference can be an insurmountable obstacle."

George nodded, took a sip of his drink, frowned thoughtfully. "Yeah, but that's not the only reason an E.T. marriage breaks up. Hell, Pi Alpha Alpha has an atmosphere and ecology 93% analogous to Homeworld —but I'd never marry one of their women."

"Pi Alpha Alpha is a lovely planet. I understand that the mating flights of the winged wisps are lovely to see and even more thrilling to be a part of. And the Matriarchy encourages inter-marriage. Off-worlders are eagerly welcomed, and if you can't fly, they'll even supply the grav-belt for the wedding night—"

"Tri-Mach," interrupted George wearily. "It's obvious that you know little of human psychology."

"That's why I am discussing this matter with you, George. I fail to understand why marriage with a winged wisp would be impractical. It is said to be a most soul-satisfying experience—"

"Hmp," said George. "A winged wisp is a most *un-*

female creature, with very *un*female sex organs. They lay their eggs inside the bodies of the males. When the egg hatches, the father carries the slug-child while it grows inside him. Oh yes, and while it grows it also devours the father's innards. Until the father dies; that is; at which point the thing gorges itself, encapsulates, hibernates, and metamorphoses into a pre-adolescent. Sorry, that's not for me, Tri-Mach. If I'm going to be a parent, I'd prefer to do it the more traditional way."

Tri-Mach nodded his eyestalks. "Yes, I understand. A conflict in sexual and parental drives, coupled with the basic survival instinct. Yes, yes, George, I understand now. Differences in inherent psychologies and cultural drives can prevent a marriage from succeeding."

"You're trying to simplify everything, Tri-Mach," George accused. "One can have exactly the same drives as one's mate—and things still won't work out. For instance, I was once married to one of the Gorgons of Golias. They call them that because their sensory tendrils grow in a fringe around the top of their heads."

"I am familiar with the species," Tri-Mach noted.

"Well, Mettisoi was one of the most beautiful Gorgons I'd ever seen—such tendrils—"

"Mettisoi? Her name? What does that mean?"

"Oh, well, there's no exact human equivalent, but on Golias it's a very beautiful, very romantic name. Something like, 'Voice of the Bull, Soul of the Toad.' "

"A beautiful name."

"English doesn't do it justice. Anyway, when we began to suspect we had something going, we knew we wanted to be sure. By then, I'd already been burned a couple of times, and she—well, anyway, we paid a visit to InterMate and ran our psyches through Comp-Central."

"And—?"

"And came up with an 83% match. Pretty good, huh? Especially for an interspecie marriage."

"Then I don't understand. The marriage should have been successful."

"It should have been, yes," George agreed. "Our drives were similar and compatible—but, hell man, she'd like to have killed me with her demands. Seven, eight, ten times a night she'd want to have sex. She was insatiable. The marriage lasted less than a week."

"Tsk tsk," said Tri-Mach.

"She claimed that I didn't love her, that I was impotent. I argued that she was a nymphomaniac. Yet, the damned machine (no offense intended) had said we were compatible."

"Obviously," said Tri-Mach, "the analysis of the data was incorrect, a failure to realize the difference in degree. Could it have been a human error?" Tri-Mach suggested gently.

"I don't know. Whatever it was, I had to find out the hard way."

"Then, there is no simple answer?"

George took another sip of his drink, thought about it for a long moment. Tri-Mach quickly scanned the other customers at the bar, then returned his attention to George, who was speaking again. "I'm not sure I could agree with you on that completely. I know exactly why I lost my fifth (or was it my sixth) wife. No ifs, ands, or buts."

"Oh? Why?"

"Give me a refill on that Sirian Slush and I'll tell you." George held out his glass. Tri-Mach took it with one of his six multi-jointed arms. Once more the robot began its routine of strobing, stroking, stoking, swizzling, swirling, shaking, scalding and skreexling. "What was your fifth (or was it your sixth?) wife like?"

Actually, Tri-Mach already knew; he had consulted

the GalacCentral Index on George N-Kolpus, Home-worlder; but he asked the question to keep him talking.

George sighed, something he did often when he thought of his many wives. "A mech. I had her built entirely to my specifications. She was going to be my ideal woman. But when she was completed, she decided to look for the ideal man. She ran off with an InterBem programmer and I haven't heard from her since." George sighed again. "I never even had a chance to name her."

Tri-Mach wiped a drop of lubricant from one of his eyestalks; that was a neat touch too, and it too went into his repertoire. He set George's drink in front of him. "How sad—and yet, I certainly must commend her taste."

George ignored him, concentrated on his drink. "After that," he continued, "I went back to Home-world. Thought I could get away from it all by going back to where it started. Or something like that."

"And?"

"And that's where I met Jenny Ondoline, a native of Bilversob 91."

"And you married her?"

"Of course. Don't I always?"

Tri-Mach remained discreetly silent.

"Jenny was an Earth name she took because she liked the sound of it, but Ondoline was her real name. It meant 'Silver Needles Making Golden Bites of Love, Devouring Delicate Morsels of Pleasure.' "

"A lovely name—"

"I thought so too. Indeed, I thought that this time, perhaps this time, this one would be the one to work out—but, as always, the sex thing got in the way."

"You weren't able to satisfy her?"

"That's putting it mildly. I discovered a very interesting thing about the women of Bilversob 91."

"And that is ... ?"

"Teeth."

"Teeth?"

"Yes, teeth. They have teeth."

"But, most humanoid life forms have—"

"Not in this location, they don't."

"Oh."

"My not being a member of the same race, I couldn't guarantee that a certain portion of my anatomy would regenerate every eighteen days—and I certainly wasn't going to find out by experimentation. The science of prosthetics isn't *that* good yet. And—well, you get the idea."

"Yes, I do," Tri-Mach oozed solicitously. "Castration fear. You have led a very uneven life, George."

"I know. But I am sure that somewhere in this wide wide Galaxy there is the perfect mate for me. And if there isn't—I'm going to go down trying."

"I'm sure you will," the robot noted.

"The thing is, it's always the fact that we're sexually incompatible that breaks us up. Well, almost always— there was one, her name was G'llumph."

"G'lumph?"

"G'llumph. The accent is on the second syllable. It meant 'Mottled Mass of Amorphous Pink.' "

"A lovely name."

"An even lovelier creature."

"Where was she from?"

"Steef, the sponge planet."

"Oh? Then she was a pseudo-plod. A most interesting life form."

"Just a big old blob of protoplasm; not much to look at you'd think," said George, "but she was such a big old *beautiful* blob of protoplasm! Ahh, now *there* was a good lay! We didn't even have enough money for a bed; but that was okay, there was more room on the floor. Besides, if you know anything about pseudo-plods, you'll know they don't use them anyway."

Tri-Mach nodded knowingly.

"When you marry a pseudo-plod, Tri-Mach, you don't worry about such things as beds. You just lay down and roll around in it—yum! No need even to take off your clothes; she could absorb them right off your back. Mmm! She had the most actively pneumatic protoplasm I've ever been loved by. She just flowed in and around and all over and—well, I can't describe it. It was like returning to the womb, but a very sexy womb." George took a drink. "I still think of her. Of all the girls I've ever loved, she was the best in bed—hell, she *was* the bed. She was fantastic—she— I'm sorry. I've said too much already."

"No, it's all right, George. Go on. Finish your story."

George took another drink. "Well, it was working out so beatifully, I couldn't believe it. I thought at last I'd found the one. I'd been in love too many times to be mistaken. This was the real thing. I actually looked forward to coming home every night from the yaste-farms—I didn't even bother to shower with the other men—I knew G'llumph was waiting for me and she would absorb the excess yaste right off my body. She so liked those little snacks I brought her. It was such a pleasure to spend a simple quiet evening at home, just wrapped up in one another."

"But—?" prompted Tri-Mach.

"But? Oh, well, she began to talk about children."

"Children?"

George nodded. "And you know how pseudo-plods reproduce, don't you? By fission. That would have left me with no wife and two daughters. Actually, either one of them, or both, would still have been my

G'llumph, but a man can't do anything with his own daughters! That would have been—that would have been—unthinkable, you know. And besides, it would have meant choosing one over the other."

"Yes," said the robot. Actually, he didn't know, but it was a colloquialism, and he accepted it as such. Discreetly, he let the matter drop.

"And the way she wanted to— She said she would have to reach a certain critical size to initiate fission, which meant taking on a certain mass of food—and if I really wanted to be the father of my children, then I could— That is— Well, she would— I tell you, Tri-Mach, I really loved that woman. I considered it for a long time. It would have been one hell of a way to go; but after a bit, I realized it was the same as marrying a winged wisp. The process might have been different, but the result was the same." George finished his drink. "So I told her, no children."

"And she left you?"

"Oh, no. We were too much in love. She seemed to accept my decision and never brought the subject up again. Or so I thought. But I could sense her getting edgy and nervous. She so wanted children, and I couldn't give them to her—or rather, she couldn't give them to me.

"Well, you know how pseudo-plods eat, of course. They just wrap themselves around their food and absorb it. And when they get mad at another pseudo-plod and have a fight—well, they try to absorb their enemies. And when two pseudo-plods are settling a quarrel, they're really eating each other simultaneously."

"Hm," said Tri-Mach, giving interested response number seven.

"Any way, what it is, is that every time there's a difference of opinion, the opponents *absorb* their differences. Literally. Now, I wasn't completely sure that this was what was going on in her mind, but I had the feeling that she was planning to surprise me and go ahead anyway—you know how women are—and I doubted that I would survive such an experience. Supposedly, she wasn't planning to ingest my brain tissue, but how could I be sure she wouldn't get carried away in the heat of passion? No matter how good her intentions were, what if she couldn't differentiate between one kind of food and another? Well, she got upset with me, said I didn't trust her any more, and wouldn't I please come to her so we could kiss and make up? I told her she could go fission. I was leaving. She did and I did."

Tri-Mach considered wiping away another simulated tear, decided it would be ostentatious, instead asked, "So what are you going to do now?"

"Sit here and wait," George replied.

"You have no plans for the future?"

"Marriage, probably."

"Oh, really?" Tri-Mach spread his eyestalks in surprise. "Who is the lucky—"

"I don't know yet. That's what I'm waiting for."

The robot hummed thoughtfully. "I suppose I shouldn't butt in like this, George, but I have been analyzing your personality, your psychology, your needs, your drives, and so on—" He paused delicately.

"Yes?"

"Perhaps it is not my place—that is, I'm really not programmed as a matchmaker—but I would like to introduce you to someone. I think perhaps there is a chance that the two of you might have a mutual interest. At least, it might be worth a try."

George shrugged. "Why not? What have I got to lose? Who is she?"

Tri-Mach gestured toward the other end of the bar. "A native of Wildebeest III." George looked. Sitting there was a slender and feminine-looking young thing, a lilac and lavender loveliness, gently clothed in wispy veils of cerulean and scented with the subtle aura of rare blossoms.

"She moves like a poem," breathed George. "Like a breeze through a willow tree, like a spider-web veil, like a— Tri-Mach, you must introduce me." George was already moving down the bar, his past loves forgotten.

"Excuse me, uh Miss—may I buy you a drink?"

A smile, sweet as honey; eyes flickering across George's even features. "Why yes, thank you."

"Uh, my name is George. And you are—"

"Gita." A voice like a sigh.

"Beautiful," breathed George. "Simply beautiful."

Gita fluttered long eyelashes at him and laughed softly.

"Gita, Gita . . ." George was entranced. "Your eyes are so beautiful, so purple. Your skin, so lovely, so blue—"

"You are most handsome yourself," Gita breathed, shaking long veils of hair around her shoulders. Her eyes glowed with interest.

George slid his hand along the bar, gently stroked Gita's slender wrist. He wasn't rebuffed. Their eyes met, a penetrating never-ending deep and searching look. "Gita, you're beautiful—my Gita—"

"George—my George—"

Two weeks later, the lovers, George and Gita, returned to THE BOTTOM HALF OF INFINITY, BAR AND GRILL and announced, "Tri-Mach, we're going to be married."

The robot spread his eyestalks in happy surprise. "Congratulations. Then everything is working out for you?"

"It couldn't be better," Gita giggled and cuddled closer to George's arm.

"Tri-Mach, I don't know how to thank you. You knew exactly what I needed. I was a fool ever to mess around with non-humanoid life forms. Gita and I are perfectly matched."

Gita blushed.

"Then, the uh, sex factor is working out? I wasn't quite sure—"

George looked a bit sheepish. Gita smiled: "It is simple. It is so much like Earthworlders that it could not be more so."

"Do you mind," asked Tri-Mach, "if I ask how you do *it?*"

"It is simple," said Gita. "The two lovers lie face to face, with their arms around each other, and their organs unite and mingle."

George put his arm around his wife. "Gita's organs are two flaccid spongelike veils which become fluid and active during intercourse. Quite compatible with the terrestrial male," George noted. His attitude was detached, almost professional.

Tri-Mach beamed. "Then I'm delighted that the two of you have exchanged names. George, what is your Wildean name?"

George smiled. "On Wildebeest III, I am known as Kisteen."

"And Gita?" the robot asked. "What is your new name? Your Earth name?"

Gita smiled, put an arm carefully around George's waist. "Ralph," she said.

Battle Hum and the Boje

The sound was bad right from the beginning. The notes just drooled out of the horn and lay there. No life to them.

So I did a fanfare *shtick* and passed the melody over to Loamy, the man with the bass. He played with it for a bit while Earlie, the drummer, embroidered the edges with a *ra-tata-ra-tata* on the snare. But their hearts weren't in it either, and the audience knew it.

It was a bad night all around. Usually an audience will sit and listen; but when they know the stuff is bad, they just sit. And that's what they were doing tonight. Just sitting.

A couple of months or years ago I would have dismissed it without a thought. "It's just the war. They're down because it isn't going well."

But the war had been going on too long for it to have any meaning any more. It could no longer affect our lives. It was part of living. Like breathing. One didn't think about it; you just accepted it. So it wasn't the war.

And it wasn't that we weren't trying either—I knew we were. We'd started out as high as ever, ready to make music the best we could. But by the time we were into the third number we knew something was wrong. If an audience doesn't warm up by then, they're not going to warm up at all. We might as well have been playing to a graveyard.

The whole thing was a contact bummer. We couldn't warm them up and we couldn't keep ourselves going without the feedback from them. So we started downhill, and the worse we got, the worse they got. And all the way down, we could see it happening. We knew *what* was happening and *why* it was happening, but we couldn't do a thing about it.

And that's a frightening thing to any horn man, the contact bummer. You know it's possible for a good piece of horn to lift an audience right out of their seats and keep them rising—but when it works the other way around it can make you stop and think, *am I losing it?*

Bojo was standing by the edge of the stage; he looked like he wanted something, so I signaled the others to keep it going or wrap it up without me. It wasn't a bad set, but it wasn't good either. (Like the ever-present war, it had lost all its meaning—but it just kept on going. . . .) Loamy flashed me a grin, a we'll-go-down-fightin' look, as I stepped past him and down off the stand next to the Boje. "What's up?"

He shook his head. "Nothing. But I'm gonna wrap it up early tonight."

"Huh—"

"It's not your fault," he cut me off. "You and the boys have been on top of it all the way in. I just feel like wrapping it early. Do one more set for me and that'll be it."

"Sure. Why not?" I shrugged. Sometimes Bojo doesn't make sense, but I'd give my horn for him if he asked— and that should give you some idea how much I think of the Boje. "You name it. What do you want to hear?"

There was a funny look on his face. "The *Battle Hum.*"

"Huh? Hey, are you feeling all right?"

"Yeah, sure. Just play it, huh?"

I shrugged again. "Whatever you want." I almost added, "Sarge," but decided that the Boje was in no mood to be kidded about his army career. Okay, if it was the *Battle Hum* he wanted, the *Battle Hum* he'd get.

The *Battle Hum* is an experiment that failed—but it failed so successfully that we've never been able to live it down. A while back, we'd given some thought to breaking out of the jazz idiom and had tried to do some of the folk-rock stuff that was so popular (and commercial). Not the head music and the so-called protest stuff; instead, we had thought we could trace our musical origins, and that sort of thing.

But the jazz was so firmly rooted in our blood that most of what came out sounded too much like a blend of both and not enough of either to be distinctive.

We'd just about come to the conclusion that it wouldn't work when one night Bojo suggested we try doing the *Battle Hymn of the Republic.* (He'd been in a funny mood that night too. It might have been the night Kennedy died. The second one.) I gave him a funny look, "Your good conduct medal acting up again?"

He smiled. I expected him to reply, "I wish I'd had you in my unit, Duff. You wouldn't be so flip." But instead he murmured, "Try it. See what it sounds like."

The boys and I exchanged a glance. Why not? What have we got to lose? We did it as a lark, playing with it, noodling the various themes back and forth, exploring the nuances of its melody.

Of course, when we were through with it, it sounded

nothing like the original; long moody passages of blues alternated with blaring horn solos. I confess no great fondness for the traditional military version, and when trapped in a piece of music like that, I begin inventing. I used both clarinet and horn in it. I did one passage with a bugle, and once found myself wondering what a trombone would do.

Anyway, it turned out to be our most successful experiment, but it could just as well have been a failure. There was no place to go with it, and it was a constant reminder of a whole set of experiments that hadn't worked.

And try as we could to bury it, it refused to lie down and stay dead. Requests for it popped up regular—everything from Lincoln's Birthday to the Kennedy Assassinations. Boje would ask for it every July 4th. That was the only time his taste descended to that of the marks. He loved it as much as they, even though he knew we hated to do it. He didn't ask us to do it very often, though.

Loamy faded out with the bass and Earlie put a stinger on the end with the drums. Almost immediately the Boje was up on the stage, which wasn't like him. He doesn't step on a man's applause, but he had a look on his face like I hope never to see again. Like death it was.

He held up his hands and cut the audience off short —not that they would have applauded much more anyway, but Bojo wasn't waiting to see. "Ladies, Gentlemen," he began. He paused, and for a second I thought he was going to say something else, but he seemed to change his mind and said, "There will be only one more set tonight and then we will be closing early."

A disinterested murmur from the audience—they really didn't care. Only the hope of some excitement in an otherwise meaningless evening caused them to wonder aloud.

I passed Bojo as he stepped down, but he didn't say anything. The boys looked at me curiously. I shrugged in reply: "The *Battle Hum*."

Loamy started to protest, but I cut him off. "For the Boje. And tighten up on that bass, you're getting sloppy."

"S'posed to be sloppy," he muttered, and I shot him a look that said, "Not in this group, it's not."

We started off easy, sort of snuck up on it slowlike. Began with a slow steady drumbeat, low and slow, one hundred to the minute, and after a bit Loamy was under it all just hinting at something else with a bass that was almost sullen.

Jack on the piano kept waiting for me to cue him in, but I held back. There was something in the sound of the bass that I hadn't heard before. At first I wondered how Loamy was doing it, but then I realized he wasn't. A glance at him told me he was playing as sloppy as ever.

But there was *something* there. Something I couldn't quite place, something that didn't belong in the sound. Offhandedly, I'd have guessed we were picking up some kind of harmonic off Boje's fancy glasswork, but this was deeper than any echo had a right to be.

I let it be and cued Jack in on the piano, but softly. He began with a slow steady alternation of notes, only hinting at the theme to come, but not giving it away. The whole thing was very dark, very sombre; the audience still did not know what we were doing, and for the first time that night they were paying attention.

If I'd thought the piano was going to cover up that echo, I was wrong. It only seemed to heighten its effect. It was more distinct than ever—but I still couldn't make it out. It wasn't unpleasant though; in fact, it might almost have been a perfect counterpoint.

I picked up the horn, even started to place it to my lips, then changed my mind. Clarinet. Only clarinet would do for this. It's the only real instrument for me. It's the soul stick. It can have a sweet caressable sound, like fresh milk being poured into a saucer—or it can blare out with all the harsh frenzy of a two-dollar whore. It's the closest I've ever come to *the* sound.

I eased in slowly, softly, with the gentle stroking of air that only the clarinet can do just so. The very name *clarinet* seems to hint at what the instrument can do. I could hear the words in my head as I began, like from a distant choir—an all male chorus, "Mine eyes have seen the glory of the coming of the . . ."

I found myself thinking about the war again, wondering what it must be like to be on the other side, wondering how it would be to be one of the enemy—

Abruptly, I felt sorry for them, for they were doomed and didn't know it. We always won. Always. Because we were right. And then I felt sorry for us too—what if we were wrong and didn't know it?

I shoved the thought out of my head, put my mind back on the music. Like the blues, slow and muted, the melody was sobbing through the room, its very slowness a sign that it could not last. For when the Duff plays the *Battle Hum,* it's anything but soft and subtle. We only start out that way. It's a battle hum and it's gotta be played that way, loud and brassy.

It's a sound that has to be heard above the din of battle, above the dull thunder of the bombs, the agonized screams of the dying. It has to grab the men, lift them, pick them up and hurl them back into battle. It's got to be so vivid that you forget the smell of your blood, the pain of your torn flesh, your fears of death and damnation, and nothing must exist for you but the sound and the glory, and you rise and keep going. And keep on going. For the sound, the beautiful sound.

Earlie picks up the pace then, and Loamy adds overtones and things with the bass. Jack starts slipping in some extra notes, and before we realize it Earlie has eased us into a whole new tempo, twice as fast as before, and then I'm blowing out my guts and my mind at the same time. Nothing exists but the clarinet and the sound—and somewhere on the fringes of my existence, the piano, the bass and the drums all combining to make *that* sound. *The* sound.

Except this time it was different. Over it, under it, around it, was this *other* sound. That echo I couldn't quite place. But not an echo—a harmony? Something. It filtered in through the edges of our sound, diffracted and deflected—but always the same and always distant. And never quite drowned out.

A sound like listening.

We build to a crashing, thundering crescendo, and then suddenly—

—we stop, leaving only the slow steady drumbeat, still one hundred to the minute. Right back where we started. It rolls through the room that is still reverberating with a thunder that refuses to die out. Slowly we come back in with the theme, *"Glory, glory, hallelujah . . ."* Soft and almost silent, just a hint, and let it hang in the air. Not even a repeat, just slip through it once and let it fade out.

It takes a while for them to realize we've finished, but when they do it shatters their minds, and then they're applauding, more than they've done all evening. "Okay, boys. Good job. Pack 'em up."

It didn't take the boys long. There was none of the usual byplay and kidding on the stand. *Battle Hum* does that, leaves us feeling as if we've crashed. Another reason I don't like it. Music should leave you feeling up.

Abruptly I remembered that *other* sound and asked if anybody else had heard anything strange, but they just shrugged and shook their heads.

"You mean a kind of twangy thing?" Jack asked. "It could have been the piano. It seemed—"

"Uh uh." He hadn't heard it. If he had, he'd have known what I meant. Either I was the only one who'd heard that *other* sound, or no one else wanted to admit it.

What was left of the audience was just filtering out. Bojo was at the bar, resting his head in his hands, half a beer sitting warmly in front of him. "G'night, Boje," I said as I passed.

"Wait a minute, Duff," he mumbled.

I paused while he fumbled in his sweater pocket. He thrust a wad of bills at me. "Hey, what's this? Payday isn't until Friday."

"Uh uh, it's today. Tonight's your last night."

"Huh—? Hey, now look, Boje. You and I are friends. I know we were a little loose on the first few sets, but give us a chance."

He shook his head. "That's not it, Duff. Your guys are all right, and if you'll count that you'll find it's for a complete gig. It's just that this—" He paused to swallow. "This is my last night too. I'm closing it up."

Huh?"

He shoved the bills at me again; I was too dumbfounded not to take them. "It's all there, Duff—and for the two extra weeks too." He smiled. "The two extra you always con me into. I'm sorry you won't be here to play them. I like your style." Then he turned back to the bar and stared into his beer. It had a sickly green cast; the glow of the black light did that to it.

I could see that he didn't want to talk. I hefted my two instrument cases and left.

Outside on the street, the boys gave me that look— as if I hadn't been telling them everything. I shrugged it off, the way I shrugged everything off. "He has his moods," I explained. "Music does that to him. Even ours." I said it without smiling. It wasn't funny. "I'll call Bill tomorrow, see if he can get us anything."

"Hmp," snorted Loamy. "He'd book us into Hell if there was a percentage in it."

Loamy and Jack walked off. Earlie gave me a wave and crossed the street to his battered Ford. It wasn't even one o'clock yet and already the streets were deserted. A light mist gave the buildings a feathery look, and the street lights were haloed.

I turned and started walking.

And suddenly it was all clear.

Why there was no traffic, no people about.

The tank sat in the middle of the intersection, a giant beetle, squat and ugly. Three soldiers in baggy-green uniforms eyed me uncuriously. Down the boulevard, I could see other tanks, and scattered among them, the lean hungry jeeps, the pale shadowy figures of men. And all had that air of watchful readiness.

So it was over.

Sometime during the evening, the whole thing had ended. We had lost it. Without even noticing.

The great tanks had rolled into our city and taken up their positions and we hadn't even noticed.

It's one thing to see it in a picture: twenty-one inches of glowing red-green-blue dots, and all so distant and far away you know it doesn't really have anything to do with you.

And it's another thing to see it in person. The hulking metal shapes, monstrous and brooding—they had one purpose and one purpose only. The sullen power of great violence forged into shapes of metal is always ugly.

There was nothing I could do. I could stand and look, or I could go home.

I went home.

And all the way, every step of the way, the questions gnawed at the edges of my mind.

Why? Why?

Somehow, irrationally, I had the idea that it was ultimately all my fault. I personally was the one responsible. Something I had done had brought this about.

But I hadn't done *anything*.

Had it been that? While I had concerned myself with providing diversions for the affluent, had others been looking hungrily after that same damned affluence? Hadn't I known? Hadn't I seen?

And most of all, why hadn't I cared?

But, no. I'd concerned myself with my music as if that had been the sole portion of my life, and not just the soul portion. While I had been blowing—no, while *we* had been blowing our hearts out in the Boje's dingy little rathole cafe, our country had had its heart blown out by our indifference.

By my indifference. Where had I been when these ugly men in their baggy-green uniforms had come rolling silently into the world?

Where? Providing casual entertainment for the casual who didn't care.

While the fat roly-poly Romans had gone to their circuses and discotheques, the lean hungry barbarians from the north had moved in. The Roman Empire never fell—it was given away.

Oh, sure—we had known there was a war on. It was in all the papers. But wars were always fought "over there." Never "over here." So we worried about and watched that other war, the far away one, and forgot about the one that was taking place right here at home.

How does it feel to be the fool, Duff? How does it feel to know that you're one of the reasons the streets are no longer ours?

And the city was longer ours. Nothing was *ours*.

The soldiers ignored me. They were as bored as the audiences I played for. And for the same reasons, too. They knew I would cause them no excitement, no reason even to straighten up. No nothing. So why strain? Why bother?

It was going to be a peaceful occupation for the United States.

The poet had been right. Not with a bang, but a whimper.

I went home, my footsteps echoing hollowly off the sidewalk and the mocking walls of the city.

It was as if we had been suddenly killed, but didn't know it yet. We went through the motions of living while in the process of dying.

The world went impossibly on. Cats padded through the garbage, dogs lifted their legs to telephone poles and trees, cars continued to mutter obscenely through the streets. Impossibly, maddeningly normal.

As if they had every right to go on existing even though the world had changed hands in the night.

There was even a sense of relief in the air, that at last it was finally here and over with. After one startled disoriented moment, the people came back into the streets to again tend to their personal businesses. Well, they're here, they said, and it's not as bad as we'd thought it would be. After all, they're only human beings, just like us. . . .

. . . *shadowy gray and ghostly silent, they sat on*

their street corners, polishing their guns and waiting.
But they're only human beings. Just like us . . . .
The new government was named.
Life went on.
The same companies sent out the same bills on the same letterheads.
And always, the same people paid.

But Bojo's stayed closed, and we were out of work. Again.
And we stayed out of work. Other places began to close up too. Not all like Bojo's. And not all for the same reasons. Some were better, some worse. But all were closed.
The fools were out of work now. They'd done their job. No—*we'd* done our job. Indeed, done it well. There was no need for us any longer. We'd diverted the attention of the landlords long enough for the looters to take possession. And now that the looters had what they wanted, they had no more need for fools.
Most of the nightspots in town simply stopped opening. One night they'd be playing to a half-empty house and the next the doors would remain shut and nobody would be playing at all.
The stage shows closed; the movie theatres too, for a while, then they re-opened with new films and unfamiliar titles. Only the bars remained unaffected, except that prices went up. A new liquor tax, they said.
Everywhere the casual entertainments disappeared. Withered away and died. Their purpose had been fulfilled.
I sat in the back of a darkened theatre, shadows flickering on the screen—shadows of the shadows that moved through the streets outside—and mourned the loss of a world I had helped to forsake.

The colors seeped out of the life, and the world was gray.

And the horror of it was that too soon we would grow used to this, our new way of life, grow complacent with the fact that the new was comfortably reminiscent of the old. After all, weren't we still eating regular, still wearing warm clothes and sleeping between clean sheets? It'd be only a matter of time till we forgot that there had once been *more* to life than this.

What *more?* I wondered. What *more?* Had there ever really been anything *more* to my life than this? Had there? Not for me, there hadn't. So why was I complaining?

What about the others? Didn't they realize that something was missing?

No, I guess not. Nobody seemed to mind. Nobody at all.

Oh, they grumbled a little bit at first—it's quite necessary to grumble when there's any kind of change in your cage, it's a fact of life—but like the weather, nobody even *tried* to do anything about it.

We've had enough war, they said. It's time for peace.

. . . *The peace of the grave, the soft and restful, quiet grave.* . . .

It was the Boje who refused to lie down and stay dead. So it had to be the Boje who was the first to die.

I should have been standing with the Boje. We all should have. But we weren't; we just stood by and watched while he and a few others organized their rally. Frozen with indecision, I shrugged off his request for help: "Uh, I can't do it, Boje. You understand . . ."

"Yes, I do. I'm sorry I bothered you, Duff."

"Oh, that's okay. Listen, if there's anything else you need—" But the phone was a dead instrument in my hand.

I went anyway. Just to watch. I hung back at a distance and watched from the other side of the street. Far enough away so as not to be confused with them.

They had a small crowd, probably not more than two or three hundred. Once I thought I saw Earlie. He turned and waved at me, but I shook my head. He seemed to shrug and disappeared back into the crowd. They stood milling nervously in front of Bojo's place, waiting for someone to give them direction. Boje was there in the thick of it. He didn't see me; he was hassling with someone about something.

Finally, fifteen minutes late, they started. Boje brought out a huge flag; I wondered where he'd gotten it. It looked almost too heavy to handle, and he had to pass it to a taller, stronger man. Even so, it ended up they needed two people to carry it.

They began to move slowly down the center of the street. Startled drivers pulled over to the side to let them pass. Others halted in amazement, and the crowd simply flowed around their cars. Heads sticking out of windows, the drivers gaped.

Some hastily parked their vehicles and scrambled to follow the Boje's group. Curiosity mostly. They too wondered who would be so foolish as to do this kind of thing in this new kind of day. Others, annoyed, threw their cars into reverse, backed away and disappeared down side streets.

I followed the group, still keeping my distance.

By the time they reached their destination, the big intersection at the center of the city, the crowd had grown to four hundred, maybe a little more. They flooded over the sidewalks and filled the street—loose knots of people, individual stragglers, curious by-standers.

They filled the intersection. Cars and buses came to a grudging halt, and after a few minutes their passengers spilled wonderingly from them to join the crowd. Meanwhile, Bojo was clambering onto the hood of a car, Earlie's battered Ford, it looked like. Someone put an electric bullhorn into his hands.

There was scattered applause as he began to speak, but it died away quickly; the people wanted to hear what he was saying. "My fellow countrymen," he began, and his words sounded silly. And feeble. But with the bullhorn, they cut through the air sharp and clear, only to be cluttered by their own echoes bouncing back off the buildings. Still, if one strained, one could make out their meaning.

"My fellow countrymen," he repeated. "We're here today to . . . to wash our flag. It's been disgraced." No reaction from the crowd. "Our country has been taken from us. Yes, taken." He paused again, still unsure of himself. The crowd waited, still not sure of itself. "But that is not the disgrace," he continued. "Our shame is that we have *let* them take it."

Again he paused, looking around for some reaction. Here and there, one or two people started to applaud, but quickly stopped when they saw they were alone. The crowd continued to wait. Bojo put the bullhorn to his lips again. "While we sat by and did nothing, they took over. And it's time we took it back—or at least showed them that we are not going to give away anything so precious as our freedom."

Still no reaction from the crowd. Bojo swallowed nervously and went on. "Do you know how many men died in the revolution that gave birth to this country? Do you know how many men have died since then to preserve the ideals on which it was founded?" He looked out over the crowd, letting the question sink in.

"No," shouted a self-appointed spokesman. "How many?"

The Boje looked momentarily at a loss. "Uh, I don't know," he admitted. "I'm not a historian. I'm only a cafe owner." Laughter, harsh and mocking, drowned out the rest of his words. I gritted my teeth, looked at my shoes. Oh, Boje, Boje, Boje.

He waited until the noise died down and began again, this time a little angrier. "But I can tell you this much—it wasn't enough!" The crowd went silent.

"If more of our men had been willing to fight for those ideals—those ideals they said they believed in— there wouldn't be soldiers in our streets today!"

"Yeah! You tell 'em!" someone in the back shouted. This was followed by a couple of other "yeah"s and a scattering of applause.

Boje smiled appreciatively, gave a nervous wave. "Okay, I will. Uh, I'm sure there's not a person in this crowd who hasn't been touched by the war. We all know someone who's been fighting for us. Probably we all know someone who's been killed while fighting for us. Are we going to turn to them now and say, 'Thanks a lot, but it wasn't worth the fight'?"

"It's our turn now. It's our turn to show that we believe in the battles we've been sending men off to fight for the past two hundred years. It's time for us to show that these men haven't died in vain."

He opened his mouth to go on, but the crowd interrupted him with their applause. Boje waited, surprised, but standing tall, growing taller every second.

"If we don't take up our fight now, it will be as if we have never existed at all, and it will make all of those other deaths meaningless. Nobody's going to give our country back to us unless we show them that we want it back. It's time to show them that we can be killed, but never defeated."

The crowd applauded that too.

And that's when the tanks moved in.

It wasn't a very good speech, and there wasn't much in it that was original; but the Boje had died for it, and that was enough.

They say that you can't fight a war unless you have a cause, and you can't have a cause unless you have a martyr to identify it with. If so, Boje had given us both. A cause and a martyr.

There was a sullen undertow of resentment afterward —a kind of "it wasn't necessary to kill him, he was harmless," attitude. After all, it wasn't if he had been planning to make any *real* trouble. He was only making a speech.

And this was followed by, "Why did they have to react so hard and fast anyway? What were they afraid of?"

"Maybe the Boje was right—maybe we should . . ."

It didn't take long for the incidents to begin. Little things, like someone spitting every time he walked past one of the ill-uniformed men. Or muttering an epithet under his breath.

And, emboldened by their success in such harmless things, there were those who dared more. It was only a matter of time until others followed the Boje. Retribution was always quick and harsh. The baggy-green uniforms brooked no disobedience.

And resentment grew. The enemy was revealing himself to be ruthless. Not benevolent at all. There were those who were surprised, more who were not. There could be no traffic with him, none whatever.

Like ghosts, flitting from person to person, the rumors rose up, murmured across the city: The enemy —yes, he was openly called the enemy now—the enemy was having too much trouble controlling the civilian population. There was talk of impressment of the young, of pass cards and controls and restrictions.

There were those who were preparing themselves for battle.

And it had taken only one incident to start it all. It didn't matter what the incident was—one would have been as good as another—but the incident that focused the mood of the people was the unnecessary death of a simple man, a man who had never done more than run a jazz cafe. And one day he had stood on a car and urged a group of other men to remember what their fathers and brothers and sons had supposedly died for.

The Boje was a veteran, so they buried him in that cemetery by the freeway, where uncurious drivers could look down and see him, just one more marker in the rows of many that flickered silently past and then abruptly were gone as each car hurtled itself up that long concrete slope into the hills. Long rows of even white markers, they sprawled across the green green field.

And at the edges were trees, tall and graceful, but giving no shelter at all. They provided shade only at the very end of the day, when the sun would filter yellow through them. Long blue-black shadows lay across the upright stones, gleaming even in the late afternoon. Here lay the seeds of man, each planted carefully in the ground, each at the proper depth, and each with a neat white marker to locate and identify it—each a seed that would never sprout, and the whole a field of ungrowing.

Bojo's marker was identical with all the rest. Nothing to say, "Here. Here is the man who stood on a car and exhorted other men." Nothing to say, "Here. Here is a man who died for his country."

But then, there was no need to say it. Each of those silent white markers indicated the same thing. Each of them said, "Here. Here is a man who has died for his country."

It was here at last that, if not in life, then in death, all men were "created" equal.

The sun disappeared below the tops of the trees and behind the houses and the hills to the west, behind the silent rushing susurrus of the nearby looming highway. I hefted the case of my clarinet and began crossing the loamy earth to where the others waited with Bojo.

It was going to be one for the Boje. He had given us our start and we couldn't allow him to be sent off without some of the music he had helped to make.

Loamy was already peeling his bass out of its cover. Earlie had only his snare drum. It was all he needed; it hung on straps from his shoulders. He had a bandage on his forehead, and for some reason I was reminded of another group, a trio, and one that had played long before I was born. Earlie looked as if he should have been flanked by a man with a flute and another with a flag.

Jack looked glum without his piano. It isn't that the piano is the only instrument he plays, but it's the only instruments he *plays*—you know what I mean. Instead, he had a portable electric organ, a poor substitute—but in his mind he had to be here, and this was the only instrument that might do.

We set up our instruments in silence. Not that there

was much to set up, or much to talk about while we did it. I fitted the pieces of my clarinet together slowly. The whole atmosphere was heavy—too heavy—and it's best to leave a man alone with his thoughts at a time like that. I tested the keys of the soul stick and then tested them again. I still wasn't sure what we should play, but I had an idea what the Boje would like. Or would have liked.

Finally, when I could delay it no longer, I blew out a Duffy squeal, my trademark—a sort of a rebel yell on the clarinet. It's kind of like saying, "Here we are and we're ready to go and tonight we don't stop until we wake the dead." I always begin a set with it. It's an attention getter.

I lowered the instrument and looked at the boys. They were easy to see in the bright moonlight. Behind them stretched the even white markers of the dead, the men who had given up their lives for their country —only to have their country given up by those who stayed behind.

There were just the four of us—and all those dead men. If I had thought this was going to be a private blowoff, I was wrong. It was as private as the main floor of Hell.

An interesting analogy that.

We started off with the spirituals—the songs from Bojo's childhood, the ones he had grown up with. We played them for the Boje and we played them simply— the way they were written—and without the little touches of style that would identify us in particular.

It was a warmup for us, and more than that, it was a way of saying, "This is God's music, boys—not ours. It's not for us to lay a claim on these. We'll play our stuff, though. You wait."

As the last notes faded into the shadows, and even as the echoes fell away, the silence returned. It was an almost silence; only the distant murmur of the highway hinted at anything more. But all else was still. They were waiting.

We lifted our instruments again. This time we were going to play *our* music. This time, Bojo would know who it was standing above him and sending the notes sobbing into the night.

"A set of three, the way the Boje liked it. *This is Your Land,* first. Then, the one about the hammer. And after that, the *Battle Hum*—and we're gonna wake the dead with that one. We're gonna do some blood stirring, an' old Boje is gonna climb right out of that grave when he hears it."

And we did.

We swung into the first one, *This is Your Land*—a song with one of those melodies that grabs you in the blood and makes it flow, a sweet and sour tingle that swells inside you until it shatters your walls and bursts out as a shout of joy.

Earlie laid into it with a bite, and Loamy found things that that bass could do that I'd never heard it do before. Jack picked it up easy and rolled the melody up and down his keyboard. He had a hornlike sound, but at the same time was soft and plaintive all around.

I picked up my stick and started hurting. It'd be nice to say how it squealed and hollered and howled, how the notes hurled themselves across the lawn, shrieking even as those white markers scraped at their sounds. But it wasn't. It wasn't like that at all, and if I had expected it to be, I was surprised.

The clarinet sobbed. It wailed; it whined—it did all the things a man wants to do and can't—because a man's not supposed to do them. So I let my soul stick cry for me instead. It did that with a passion.

Long mournful wails of melody rolled out into the

night. The warm dark air seemed to swallow the sound even as it was born. Like into a vacuum.

We played it like a dirge, and then we took out the stops and swung into a big beat sound for the close. Earlie caught fire then, and those hammering drumbeats boomed and doomed. That organ seemed to be alive, and the bass was under and around it all. It was a good one, it said what we wanted it to.

No pause and we swung easily into *The Hammer*, which I knew the Boje had always liked, and that's when I began to hear the sound. I'd heard it before, only once, but I knew I'd recognize it if I ever heard it again. It was an echo, and it wasn't. It was a distant wail, mournful and sobbing, not so much a sound as a presence.

It lay under *The Hammer* and hinted at things other than.

I tried to ignore it, tried to play above it—but it was there, and the more I played the more definite was its presence. I still couldn't identify it—it came from no instrument I'd ever heard. Except perhaps the throats of a choir, one million strong.

I tried to blank it out and concentrate on my music, but after a while it was as if a new instrument had been added. Somehow, it seemed to fit in.

The Hammer is one of the ones I like to use the horn with. There are passages where only a horn can rightly grab hold of the sound and give it that special fury. Only the horn can shriek some of those phrases at the world.

But I didn't have my horn with me that night. I had the clarinet. So we played it soft—muted it down and did it like a dirge. For Boje.

I knew Earlie was getting restless with it; he was doing things with the beat. We started climbing. (I could hear that distant choir—louder than ever now. And there were words, but too fuzzy to make out.)

We blew it out big for the close, and then the silence swept back in.

We paused then. I held my hand up—nobody say a thing—and listened.

There was nothing there. Only the quiet steady rustle of the highway, and I knew that hadn't been what I'd heard.

I looked from face to face. Sweat was dripping off Earlie, and Loamy was radiant. Jack looked exhilarated. If a cool wind whispered through the night and across our backs, we didn't feel it.

I picked up the clarinet again. And this time we were going to do the *Battle Hum*. For the Boje. For all of them.

The moon disappeared behind a cloud, and we were lost in the dark. But no matter. Earlie began with the drumbeat, one hundred to the minute, and Loamy was there with his bass tickling in on the edges. Without being told, Jack began at just the right time.

—and then as I lifted my stick, I heard it. That sound. That deep distant mournful chorus wailing . . .

A cold wind swept through me—a sudden dreadful feeling. I knew exactly what was making that sound. I knew what it was, and there was nothing I could do about it.

I closed my eyes and blew.

I submerged into that music, became lost in it, played it and became one with it. But whatever it was I did, I knew I mustn't look back. I mustn't. I was afraid of what I might see.

We played that *Battle Hum* as it had never been played before—and likely as it's never going to be heard again.

Creeping into it slowly—slow and easy—beginning

like a dirge—but not a dirge, more of a march—then picking it up, a piece here and a piece there. Loamy came in and did a bass solo based on his own counterpoint, and yet was more than that. Then, just as easily, he crept out and Jack was in there doing things that only a piano knew how to do, and I had to keep reminding myself that he didn't have one tonight. And always, Earlie was there with the drums. Always. One hundred to the minute. A march. A march and a dirge.

I waited then, waited while they played for the Boje, waited and listened as they sobbed their hearts into their sound. And I wondered all the while if they could hear it, that slow low rumbling, grumbling, from deep within the bowels of the Earth.

They must have been lost in their music, for it seemed as if I was the only one aware of the trembling beneath my feet, the fear creeping up my soul. I moistened my lips, began again to blow—blow my lungs out, trying to drown out that dreadful sound.

I played my solo to a counterpoint from Hell.

I don't remember signaling, but there was Earlie, under me with the drums, all the way, lifting and shouting and all of a sudden we were rising together. I could sense the bass—I was beyond hearing—the bass was there and adding its own mournful harmonies. And Jack was there too, sobbing into his machine.

I played on, my eyes shut tight against the night. Only the music mattered, the notes, the sound. *That* sound. That low slow rumbling grumbling. I didn't want to see. I didn't want to know what was going on in that graveyard behind me.

"Boje!" I played. "Boje! This is for you. I'm sorry I let you down, Boje! I didn't mean to and I'm sorry!"

The moon hid behind its cloud and waited. Other sounds began to add themselves. Strange sounds. I became curiously detached—caught up in the experience and yet, at the same time, aware of the totality of it all. The new sounds were proper, correct, never discordant—they seemed to point up our every meaning.

There were rustlings, as if of movement. Dead dry leathery rustlings. Silent whisperings and a shambling murmur and the sense of something passing through the night—something slow and massive and ponderously invincible rolling up and out into the world; something spread out and made up of many lesser, but no less powerful, units of itself. It whispered across the night and across our sound.

We swung into the last movement of the *Battle Hum,* a battle in itself. The clarinet shrieked. It does that on the high notes if you're not careful—but here it seemed somehow right. The bass pounded, the drums boomed and doomed, and through it all was Jack holding us somehow together. We rode through it on a cresting wave, with a whole world shouting, *"Glory! Glory! Hallelujah!"* Singing it out with the music—the *Battle Hum* crashed across our sensibilities. Only the fear of that other sound kept us from flying out into a million brilliant stars.

Under and around and through it was that rumble and rustle, that grumbling bustling tremble of something big and busy moving through the night. It was something not benevolent; it had a feeling of ruthless deliberation as it went about its business. Yet it knew we were there and never touched us. It just went on with its own fearful task, taking care not to break accidentally the spell of our sound. Something that we had awakened, but not quite unleashed.

"Boje!" I played, "Boje! This is for you. I'm sorry I let you down, Boje! I didn't mean to and I'm sorry!"

And then there was silence.

And the dawn.

The graveyard was still. The ground was smooth—unbroken and unmarked. Dew gleamed wetly on the grass, blue-green and glistening. Whatever had happened last night had not happened here.

The city was empty.

The people came out into the streets and the soldiers were—gone. Their tanks lay empty in the intersections, their rifles still leaning carelessly where they had left them, their jeeps still with motors running.

Only rarely was an empty uniform discovered—baggy-green shirt, trousers and heavy boots casually discarded as if they no longer held any meaning.

But of the soldiers, never a trace was found.

There are those who claim to know what happened. It was a strike, they say. The soldiers took off their uniforms and they were no longer soldiers, they were men again. And the men went home.

Perhaps. It is an easy explanation to accept. Perhaps it is the truth. Or perhaps—

I had said our music could raise the dead, but I had used that only as an expression. I had never thought—But we played the *Battle Hum,* and every man who had ever worn the uniform of his country had risen from his grave once more to deliver his land from her enemies.

When General Sherman said that war is hell, he was saying far more than he knew. The men that had come back could only have from one place . . . .

They say that killing is a mortal sin, that it is against the laws of God. If that is true—and I know now that it must be—if that is true, then every man who has ever taken a human life has been, from that moment on, damned for eternity. No matter how many men or nations say that it is all right for a man to take up arms against an enemy, it does not change that one basic fact —killing is a mortal sin.

And every one of those simple white markers we had stood among represents a soul condemned.

A nation had sentenced her sons to damnation so that she might survive.

There's no such thing as a "moral war."

How must those men have felt to discover that they had been betrayed? How must each have realized he could not abdicate the authorship of his own crimes? What would he feel toward the leaders of his nation— the generals, the politicians, the mothers, wives and brothers he had left behind, each urging him onward to kill in their names . . . ?

And yet—

When that same nation had been betrayed, and rough-mannered soldiers abused the citizens, those same sons had returned from Hell, once more.

Greater love hath no man?

I wonder . . . .

Is this how one repents for making war? By rising up and fighting again? By repeating the sin?

Or was it something else, some other reason that made them rise up in the night?

Could it have been to protect us from ourselves? To keep us from condemning more of our young to Hell?

Was it so that we might learn to live for our ideals instead of having to die for them?

With a Finger in My I

When I looked in the mirror this morning, the pupil was gone from my left eye. Most of the iris had disappeared too. There was just a blank white area and a greasy smudge to indicate where the iris had previously been.

At first I thought it had something to do with the contact lenses, but then I realized that I don't wear lenses. I never have.

It looked kind of odd, that one blank eye staring back at me, but the unsettling thing about it was that I could still see out of it. When I put my hand over my good right eye, I found that the eyesight in my left was as good as ever, and it worried me.

If I hadn't been able to see out of it, I wouldn't have worried. It would have meant only that during the night I had gone blind in that eye. But for the pupil of the eye to just fade away without affecting my sight at all —well, it worried me. It could be a symptom of something serious.

Of course, I thought about calling the doctor, but I didn't know any doctors, and I felt a little bit embarrassed about troubling a perefct stranger with my problems. But there was that eye and it kept staring at me, so finally I went looking for the phone book.

Only, the phone book seemed to have disappeared during the night. I had been using it to prop up one end of the bookshelf, and now it was gone. So was the bookshelf—I began to wonder if perhaps I had been robbed.

First my eye, then the phone book, now my bookshelf had all disappeared. If it had not been that today was Tuesday, I should have been worried. In fact, I was already worried, but Tuesday is my day to ponder all the might-have-beens that had become never-wases. Monday is my day to worry about personal effects (such as eyes and phone books) and Monday would not be back for six days. I was throwing myself off schedule by worrying on a Tuesday. When Monday returned, then I would worry about the phone book, if I didn't have something else of a more pressing nature to worry about first.

(I find that pigeonholing my worrying like that helps me to keep an orderly mind—by alloting only so much time to each problem I am able to keep the world in its proper perspective.) But there was still the matter of the eye, and that was upsetting me. Moreover, it was *distorting* my perspective.

I resolved to do something about it immediately. I set out in search of the phone, but somewhere along the way that too had disappeared, so I was forced to abandon that exploration.

It was very frustrating—this distressing habit of disappearing that the inanimate objects had picked up. Every time I started to look for something, I found that it had vanished, as if daring me to find it. It was like playing hide-and-go-seek, and since I had long ago given up such childish pastimes, I resolved not to encourage them any further and refused to look for them any more. (Let them come to me.)

I decided that I would walk to the doctor. (I would have put on my cap, but that would have meant looking for it, and I was afraid that it too would have disappeared by the time I found it.)

Once outside, I noticed that people were staring at me in a strange way as they passed. I realized that it must be my eye. I had forgotten about it, not realizing that it might look a bit strange to others.

I started to turn around to go back for my sunglasses, but I knew that if I started to look for them, they too would surely disappear. So I turned around and headed once again for the doctor's.

"Let them come to me," I muttered, thinking of the sunglasses. I must have startled the old lady I was passing at the time because she turned to stare at me in a most peculiar manner.

I shoved my hands into my coat pockets and pushed onward. Almost immediately I felt something hard and flat in my left-hand pocket. It was my sunglasses in their case. They had indeed come to me. It was rewarding to see that I was still the master of the inanimate objects in my life.

I took the glasses out and put them on, only to find that the left lens of the glasses had faded to a milky white. It matched my eye perfectly, but I found that, unlike my eye, I was quite unable to see through the opaqued lens. I would just have to ignore the stares of passersby and proceed directly on to the doctor's office.

After a bit, however, I realized that I did not know where I was going—as I noted earlier, I did not know any doctors. And I most certainly knew that if I started to search for the office of one, I would probably never find it at all. So I stood on the sidewalk and muttered to myself, "Let them come to me."

I must confess that I was a little bit leery of this

procedure—remembering what had happened with the sunglasses—but in truth, I had no alternative. When I turned around I saw a sign on the building behind me. It said, "Medical Center." So I went in.

I walked up to the receptionist, and I looked at her. She looked at me. She looked me right in the eye (the left one) and said, "Yes, what can we do for you?"

I said, "I would like to see a doctor."

"Certainly," she said. "There goes one down the hall now. If you look quickly, you can catch a glimpse of him. See! there he goes!"

I looked and she was right—there *was* a doctor going down the hall. I could see him myself. I knew he was a doctor because he was wearing golf shoes and a sweater; then he disappeared around a bend in the corridor. I turned back to the girl. "That wasn't exactly what I meant," I said.

"Well, what was it you meant?"

I said, "I would like for a doctor to look at me."

"Oh," she said. "Why didn't you say so in the first place?"

"I thought I did," I said, but very softly.

"No, you didn't," she said. "And speak up. I can hardly hear you." She picked up her microphone and spoke into it. "Dr. Gibbon, puh-lease come to reception. . . ." Then she put down her microphone and looked at me expectantly.

I did not say anything. I waited. After a moment, another man in golf shoes and sweater came out of one of the nearby doors and walked over to us. He looked at the girl behind the desk, and she said to him, "This gentleman would like a doctor to look at him."

The doctor took a step back and looked at me. He looked me up and down, then asked me to turn around and he looked at me some more. Then he said, "Okay," and walked back into his office.

I asked, "Is that all?"

She said, "Of course, that's all. That's all you asked for. That will be ten dollars please."

"Wait a minute," I said. "I wanted him to look at my eye."

"Well," she said, "you should have said so in the first place. You know we're very busy here. We haven't got time to keep calling doctors down here to look at just anyone who wanders in. If you had wanted him to look at your eye in particular, you should have said so."

"But I don't want someone to just look at my eye," I said. "I want someone to cure it."

"Why?" She said. "Is there something wrong with it?"

I said, "Can't you see? The pupil has disappeared."

"Oh," she said. "So it has. Did you look for it?"

"Yes, I did. I looked all over for it—that's probably why I can't find it."

"Maybe you left it somewhere," she cooed softly. "Where was the last place you were?"

"I wasn't anywhere," I said.

"Well, maybe that's your trouble."

"I meant that I stayed home last night. I didn't go anywhere! And I don't feel very well."

"You don't look very well," she said. "You should see a doctor."

"I already have," I said. "He went down that hall."

"Oh, that's right I remember now."

"Look," I said. I was starting to get a little angry. "Will you please get me an appointment with a doctor?"

"Is that what you want—an *appointment?*"

"Yes, that is what I want."

"You're sure that's *all* you want now? You're not going to come back later and complain that we didn't give you what you want?"

"I'm sure," I said. "I'm not going to come back."

"Good. That's what we want to be sure of."

By now, everything seemed to be all wrong. The whole world seemed to be slipping off sideways—all squished together and stretched out and tilted so that everything was sliding down towards the edge. So far, nothing had gone over, but I thought I could see tiny cracks appearing in the surface.

I shook my head to clear it, but all that did was produce a very distinct rattling noise—like a very small walnut in a very large shell.

I sat down on the couch to wait—I was still unable to think clearly. The fog swirled in thicker than ever, obscuring everything. Visibility had been reduced to zero, and the controllers were threatening to close down all operations until the ceiling lifted. I protested, no—wasn't the ceiling all right where it was?—but they just ignored me.

I stood up then and tried to push the ceiling back by hand, but I couldn't reach it and had to stand on a chair. Even then, the surface of it was hard and unyielding. (Although I was close enough to see that there were numerous cracks and flaws in it.)

I started to push on it again, but a strong hand on my shoulder and a deep voice stopped me. "Lay down on the couch," she said. "Just close your eyes. Relax. Lie back and relax."

"All right," I said, but I did not lie on my back. I lay on my stomach and pressed my face into the hard unyielding surface.

"Relax," she said again.

"I'll try," I said, forcing myself.

"Look out the window," the doctor said. "What do you see?"

"I see clouds," I said.

"What kind?"

"What kind???"

"Yes. What kind?"

I looked again. "Cottage cheese clouds. Little scuds of cottage cheese clouds."

"Cottage cheese clouds—?" asked the doctor.

"Yes," I said. "Cottage cheese clouds. Hard and unyielding."

"Large curd or small curd?"

"Huh?" I asked. I rolled over and looked at her. She did not have on golf shoes, but she was wearing a sweater. Instead of the golf shoes, she had on high heels. But she was a doctor—I could tell that. Her shoes still had cleats.

"I asked you a question," she rumbled in that deep voice of hers.

"Yes, you did." I agreed. "Would you mind repeating it?"

"No, I wouldn't mind," she said and waited quietly.

I waited also. For a moment there was silence between us. I pushed the silence to one side and asked, "Well, what was it?"

"I asked whether the clouds were large curd or small curd."

"I give up," I said. "What were they?"

"That's very good of you to give up—otherwise we'd have had to come in after you and take you by force. By surrendering your misconceptions now you have made it so much easier for both of us."

The whole thing was coming disjointed and teetered precariously on the edge. Bigger cracks were beginning to appear in the image, and tiny pieces were starting to slip out and fall slowly to the ground where they shattered like so many soap bubbles.

"Uh—" I said. "Uh, Doctor—there's something wrong with my eye."

"Your I?"

"Uh, yes. The pupil is gone."

"The pupil is gone from your I?" The doctor was astounded. "How astounding!"

I could only nod—so I did. (A bit too hard perhaps. A few more pieces came flaking off and fluttered gently to the floor. We watched for a moment.)

"Hm," she said. "I have a theory about that. Would you like to hear it?"

I didn't answer. She was going to tell me her theory whether I wanted to hear it or not.

"The world is coming to an end," she whispered conspiratorially.

"Right now?" I asked, somewhat worriedly. I still hadn't fed the cat.

"No, but soon," she reassured me.

"Oh," I said.

We sat there in silence. After a bit, she cleared her throat. "I think . . ." she began slowly, then she trailed off.

"That's nice," I said, but she didn't hear me.

". . . I think that the world exists only as a reflection of our minds. It exists the way it does only because that's the way we think it does."

"*I* think—therefore *I* exist," I said. But she ignored me. She told me to be quiet.

"Yes, you exist," she confirmed. (I'm glad she did— I was beginning to be a bit worried—and this was the wrong day for it. The last time I looked this was Tuesday.) "You exist," she said, "because you think you do. And the world also exists because you think it does."

"Then, when I die—the world ends with me . . .?" I asked hopefully, making a mental note not to die.

"No—that's nonsense. No sane and rational man believes in solipsism." She scratched at her eyeball with a fork and went on.

"When you die—*you* cease to exist," she said. "But

the world goes on—it goes on because everybody else who's still alive still believes that it exists. (The only thing they've stopped believing in is you.) You see, the world is a collective figment of all of our individual imaginations."

"I'm sorry," I said stiffly. "I do not believe in collectivism." I unbent a little so as to sit up. "I am a staunch Republican."

"Don't you see?" she said, ignoring my interruption. "This mass hallucination that the world is real just keeps on going because of its own momentum. You believe in it because that's the way it was when you first began to exist—that is, when everybody else first began to believe you existed. When you were born, you saw that the world followed a certain set of rules that other people believed in, so you believed in them too—the fact that you believe in them just gives them that much more strength."

"Oh," I said. I lay there listening to her, trying to figure out some way to leave gracefully. My eye was starting to hurt, and I couldn't see the ceiling any more. The fog was rolling in again.

"Look at the church!" she said suddenly.

"Huh?" I said.

"Look at the church!" she said it again, insistent.

I tried to. I lifted my head and tried to look at the church, but the fog was too thick. I couldn't even see my toes.

"Look at it," she said. *"Faith* is the basic precept of religion—faith that what they're telling you is true! Don't they tell you to have faith in the church, that faith can work miracles?!! Well, I'll tell you something —it can! If enough people believe in something, it becomes reality!"

By now, my eye was throbbing most painfully. I tried to sit up, but her strong hands held me back. She leaned closer and whispered intensely, "Yes! It's true. It is."

"If you say so," I nodded.

She went on. "Fortunately, the church long ago abandoned miracles in favor of conservatism—now, it's fighting to preserve the status quo! The church is one of the last bastions of reality—it's one of the few things holding back chaos!"

"Chaos?"

"Yes, chaos."

"Oh."

"The world is changing," she explained. "Man is changing it."

I nodded. "Yes, I know. I read the newspapers too."

"No, no! That's not what I meant! Man is changing his world unconsciously! More and more people are starting to believe that they really can change their environment—and the more they believe it, the more drastically it changes. I'll give you an example—fossils!"

"Fossils?"

"Yes, fossils. Nobody ever discovered any fossils until people started believing in evolution—then when they did start to believe in it, you couldn't turn around without tripping over fossils."

"You really believe this?" I asked.

"Yes, I do!" she said intensely.

"Then it must be so," I said.

"Oh, it is," she agreed, and I knew that she really did believe it. She made a very convincing case. In fact, the more she talked, the more I began to believe it too.

"Why did you tell me all this?" I asked.

"Because we're in great danger. That's why." She whispered fiercely, "The world isn't changing uniformly. Everybody is starting to believe in different things, and they're forming pockets of non-causality."

"Like a pimple?" I offered.

"Yes," she said, and I could see a small one forming

on the tip of her nose. "It works this way: A fanatic meets another fanatic, then the two of them meet with some other people who share the same hallucinations, and pretty soon there are a whole bunch of fanatics all believing the same thing—pretty soon, their delusions become real for them—they've started to contradict the known reality and replaced it with a node of non-reality."

I nodded and concentrated on wrapping a swirl of the fog securely around me.

"The more it changes, the more people believe in the changes, and the stronger they become. If this keeps up, we may be the only sane people left in the world—and we're in danger—"

"They're outnumbering our reality?" I suggested.

"Worse than that—all of their different outlooks are starting to flaw the structure of space! Even the shape of the Earth is changing! Why, at one time, it was really flat—the world didn't turn round until people started to believe it was round."

I turned round then and looked at her, but she had disappeared into the fog. All that was left was her grin.

"But the world is really pear-shaped," I said. "I read it in *Scientific American.*"

"And why do you think it's changing shape?" the grin asked. "It's because a certain nation is starting to believe that it's really bigger than it is. The Earth is bulging out to accommodate them."

"Oh," I said.

"It's the fault of the news media—television is influencing our image of the world! They keep telling us that the world is changing—and more and more people keep believing it."

"Well," I said. "With the shape of the world the way it is today, any change has got to be for the—"

"Oh, God—not you too! All you people keep talking about the world going to pieces—falling apart at the seams—"

And then even the grin was gone.

I was left there. I was also right. Other people had begun to notice it too. Great chunks of the surface *had* gone blotchy, and holes had appeared in it. More and more pieces were falling out all the time, but the waters had not yet broken through from the other side.

I poked my finger through one of the holes, and I could feel the soft gelatinous surface behind. Perhaps it hadn't thawed completely out yet.

So far, nothing had been accomplished about my eye —not only was it beginning to ache something fierce, but my I was beginning to twinge a bit also, and I had a feeling that that too might be going opaque.

"Have you found yourself yet?!!" one of the speakers in the park demanded. (I hadn't even looked—and remembering my previous experiences with looking for things, I certainly was not going to initiate any kind of a search.) I walked on.

Farther on, there was another speaker—this one on a soup box. "We should be thankful for this great nation of ours," the speaker woofed and tweetered, "where so many people are allowed to believe in so many different things."

I rubbed at my eye. I had an uneasy queasy feeling that great cracks were opening in the ceiling.

"Anyone can get up and speak for his cause—any group can believe in anything they choose—indeed we can remake the world if we want too! And in our own images!"

Things were teetering right and left—also write and wrong.

"But the truly great thing about it," he continued, "is that no matter how much we contradict each other, we are all working together for the common good! Our great democratic system lets us maximize our differences so that we can all compromise ourselves. Only by suggesting all the alternatives to a problem can we select the best possible solution. In the long run, this ultimate freedom and individuality will help all of us to achieve the most good for the most people!"

It sounded good to me.

When I got home, the workmen were just finishing with the wallpaper. It was amazing how solid the surface looked once all the cracks and flaws in it had been covered with a gaudy flowered facade.

I could no longer tell where the plaster had given way—and the bare surface of the understructure had disappeared into the fog. Indeed, the only thing was that the ceiling seemed to be much lower than before.

I paused long enough to stroke the cat. He waved as I came in. "Like—hello, man," said the cat. "Give me a J."

"I can't. I'm having trouble with my I."
"Well, then give me a dollar."
"What for?"
"For a trip," he said.
"Oh." I gave him a dollar, waited for the trip.

He dropped the bill into his mouth, lit it, picked up his suitcase and quickly rose to a cruising level of thirty thousand feet. Then he headed west. I did not quite understand this. The fog had gotten much worse, and the controllers were not letting any traffic through.

There had been something I had wanted to ask, but I had forgotten it. Oh, well—it couldn't have been very important. But I wish I could figure out—

The man on the TV was a Doctor. He sat on top of it with his feet dangling in front of the screen (his cleats were scratching the image) and said that the drugs were destroying the realities. Drugs could destroy a person's sanity by altering his perceptions of the world until he could no longer perceive reality at all.

"Just so long as it doesn't change what he believes in," I muttered and turned him off. Then I turned him out. It was getting late and I wanted to get some sleep. However, I did make a mental note not to have my prescription refilled. Already the wallpaper was peeling.

In fact, by now, only the framework of the structure is left, and it looks like it's made out of chocolate pudding. Maybe it is. Perhaps it *is* the drugs. Maybe they *are* altering our collective fogments—but *I* haven't noticed anything.

How We Saved the Human Race

TEST TRANS CODE ALPHA ALPHA TAU
1234567890—=
QWERTYUIOP
ASDFGHJKL+
ZXCVBNM,./
THE QUICK BROWN FOX JUMPED OVER THE
LAZY DOGS.
        END TEST
        MESSAGE BEGINS HERE
DATE/MAY-14-2037
FROM/THE UNITED STATES AMBASSADOR TO
BRAZIL
TO/ THE PRESIDENT OF THE UNITED STATES
FILE/BRZ-9076-THX
CODE/ALPHA-ALPHA-TAU/475FGH5142037
STATUS OF DOCUMENT/CLASSIFIED/TELE-
PRINTER CODE-   FGH.
MR. PRESIDENT, IN PLAIN TERMS, THE AN-
SWER IS NO. THE GOVERNMENT OF BRAZIL
ABSOLUTELY REFUSES TO RELEASE THE
BODY. THERE CAN BE NO POSSIBLE NEGOTIA-

TION ON THIS. THIS IS AN INTERNAL MATTER
—THEY CLAIM—AND NO OTHER POLITICAL
BODY WILL BE ALLOWED TO INTERVENE. OF
COURSE, THIS IS A BLATANT GRAB ON THEIR
PART, BUT THERE IS NOTHING WE CAN DO
ABOUT IT. I+M AGAINST MAKING ANY KIND
OF FLAP.

FIRST OF ALL, WORLD-WIDE OPINION GEN-
ERALLY FAVORS THE BRAZILIANS. ANY AT-
TEMPT BY US TO PRESSURE THEM WOULD
ONLY PRODUCE HOSTILE REACTIONS—AND
THAT+S THE LAST THING WE WANT NOW.

SECONDLY, THEY WANT TO TAKE CREDIT
FOR LEDGERTON+S CAPTURE. THEY FOUND
HIM AND THEY EXECUTED HIM. OR RATHER,
THEY ATTEMPTED TO. IT WAS MOST UNFOR-
TUNATE THAT THE CROWD BEAT THEM TO
IT. THERE ARE THOSE WHO SUGGEST THAT
THE POLICE DELIBERATELY LET THE LYNCH
MOB IN, BUT I WOULD DISCREDIT THAT
STORY. THEY LOST TWELVE OF THEIR OWN
MEN IN THE DISORDER.

ANYWAY, THEY WANT TO TAKE THE CREDIT,
AND FRANKLY I THINK WE OUGHT TO LET
THEM. THIS IS NOT TO SUGGEST APPEASE-
MENT, BUT THIS GOVERNMENT IS THE
FRIENDLIEST ONE BRAZIL HAS HAD IN
TWELVE YEARS AND I WOULD LIKE TO KEEP
IT THAT WAY. ANY PRESSURING ON OUR
PART WOULD DEFINITELY COOL RELATIONS.
—AND PRESIDENT GARCIA WON+T BEND TO
PRESSURE ANYWAY. POLITICAL REASONS.
THE MILITANT RIGHTISTS WOULD USE SUCH
ACQUIESCENCE AS A LEVER AGAINST HIM.—
SO . . . I THINK WE+D BETTER JUST MAKE
INEFFECTUAL NOISES FOR NOW, LOUD

ENOUGH TO PLACATE OUR OWN PEOPLE,
BUT NOT LOUD ENOUGH TO ANNOY JUAN
PABLO GARCIA.
BY THE WAY, THE BODY WILL REMAIN ON
PUBLIC DISPLAY FOR ANOTHER DAY AND A
HALF. —YES, STILL HANGING FROM THE GAL-
LOWS, BULLET HOLES AND ALL—I+VE SEEN
IT AND IT+S A GHASTLY SIGHT. NOT EVEN
LEDGERTON DESERVED WHAT THEY DID TO
HIM. YOU KNOW OF COURSE THAT THEY
CASTRATED HIM TOO.
IN ANY CASE, I HAVE IT FROM GARCIA HIM-
SELF THAT IT WILL BE TAKEN DOWN TUES-
DAY AND CREMATED. THE ASHES ARE GOING
TO BE SCATTERED AT SEA. NO, WE CAN+T
STOP THAT EITHER.
I WISH I COULD BE MORE ENCOURAGING AT
THIS TIME, BUT ALL I CAN DO IS SAY THAT
IT+S A ROTTEN SITUATION ALL AROUND.
I+LL HAVE A MORE DETAILED REPORT
LATER. DESPITE OUR CLAIMS TO THE CON-
TRARY, THERE ARE STILL TOO MANY PEO-
PLE DOWN HERE WHO BELIEVE THE WHOLE
THING WAS A C.I.A. PLOT.
FOR GOD+S SAKE, THIS IS ONE TIME WHEN
I HOPE OUR OFFICIAL POSITION COINCIDES
WITH THE TRUTH.
SINCERELY,

5-14-2057/DATELINE:BRAZIL.
CARDINAL SILENTE TODAY DEDICATED THE
MONUMENT AND ETERNAL FLAME COMMEM-
ORATING THE MARTYR DANA LEDGERTON.
THAT SUCH A HIGH-RANKING MEMBER OF
THE CATHOLIC CHURCH SHOULD TRAVEL TO
BRAZIL FOR THE CEREMONIES SUGGESTS IM-

MINENT BEATIFICATION OF THE MARTYR.
THE CARDINAL HIMSELF SAID . . .

PSYCHIATRIC INDEX REPORT
COMSKOOL TWELVE, MANWEATHER COM-
PLEX, CALIF.
May 1, 2003
Dana Ledgerton, DL 571-60-5683, age nine.

Child is unfortunately too smart and too pretty for
his own good. Male, age nine, fair skin, pale hair, thin,
under-sized for age (poor nutrition again, damn these
comskool minimums), lives in Comskool Creche. Unfortunately, subject also has advanced intelligence.
(Tests enclosed.) Presently enrolled two grades above
average for his age level. This physical discrepancy
between him and his classmates generates extreme feelings of inferiority, coupled with strong motivation to
succeed. Success on mental level increases antagonism
between himself and peers, but it is the only arena in
which he is fairly matched with his classmates. The
kid takes a lot of teasing about being a sissy, and his
sense of masculine identification is weak. I'll give odds
of ten to one that he's a fag by the time he's twenty.
RECOMMENDATIONS: None. There's nothing *we*
can do. Tough.

SUPERVISOR'S REMARKS: *Dammit, Pete! Can't
you be a little more clinical than this?* (signed) H.B.

MAY 9, 2011
LABOR POOL STATUS BOARD, CALIF. 99-5674
UNIT MONITOR FORM JHX-908
DANA LEDGERTON, DL 571-60-5683

Subject is thin, very fair, blond hair. Small for his
age. Required to perform eighteen hours of Class IV

labor per week in order to support educational demands. Assigned to manual labor in University Caf-Com. Designation: busboy.

REMARKS:

Subject discovered in Comskool Personal committing homosexual act with fellow student at age twelve. Referred to Psych-Stat who confirmed unit's sexual outlook. No recommendation made. Subject's sexual preference has no bearing on his ability to perform Class IV labor.

RECOMMENDATION:

Leave to discretion of local supervisors.

MAY 45, 2035

FROM: FIELD OPERATIVE JASON PETER
       GRIGG
TO: F.B.I. DIRECTOR WARREN J. HINDLER,
       HOOVER CENTER,
       WASHINGTON D.C.
FILE: LEDGERTON, YTR 5683

Chief,

Sorry for the sketchiness of this report; I'll have to do a complete rundown when I get back. This thing is a mess to the nth power. The Manweather records only go back twelve years. Before that, it's incomplete and often sketchy. Yest, I know that's hard to believe, but Manweather was one of the hardest hit during the sex and protein riots, and a lot of their records were wiped clean by the activists.

I'll be sending along telefaxes of the working papers, but until they arrive, here's a rough summary.

Ledgerton's birth was an accident. He wasn't wanted, not by his parents, not by the local board. When he came along, unannounced and unwelcome, the parents were sterilized and sent to Labor-Module 14, Manweather. The child was transferred to the Comskool Creche, which had only been open two years at that time and still had elbow room. However, due to shifting population pressures, Manweather became one of the densest concentrations in Calif. Within five years, it was a behavioral sink.

Competition wasn't Ledgerton's big thing. He preferred to withdraw into himself. Because his teachers and psych-stats kept telling him how smart he was and how he should be proud of himself, he became narcissistic and introverted. He took a lot of fag-baiting from his classmates, too.

There's a full psych-profile in here somewhere. I was lucky to find that. According to the shrink, "Little Dana" wasn't as self-assertive as he should have been and too many of his life-choices were made because population pressures forced him into them and he didn't feel like fighting back.

His college career tends to bear this out. He went into bio-chem strictly by accident. It was the only classification still open that he was qualified for. And it was either that or the unskilled labor pool. Nuff said about that.

MAY 24, 2014
UNIVERSITY OF CALIFORNIA AT INDIO
REAGAN HALL
FLOOR MANAGER'S MEMO
SUBJECT: REASSIGNMENT OF ROOMS

D'ana Ledgerton DL 571-60-5683 and Paul-John Murdock PJM 673-65-4532 have been reassigned (at their request) to room 12-32, the "lavender hills" section. This leaves rooms 6-87 and 7-54 with only one person in them. Immediate reassignments available for each.

MAY 3, 2015
UNIVERSITY OF CALIFORNIA AT INDIO
PSYCH-STAT REPORT, CONFIDENTIAL
SUBJECT: PAUL-JOHN MURDOCK PJM 673-65-
              4532

Subject is tall and husky. (6'1" and 161 lbs.) Fairly
well built. Dark hair, curly. Thin face. "Penetrating"
eyes—an illusion produced by deepset sockets and
heaviness of eyebrows. Prone to long periods of moodi-
ness and introspection. Theatre arts major.

He has been living for the past year with another
male student and the relationship is apparently sexual.
However, subject's emotional involvement tends to be
shallow. He has a long history of casual sexual en-
counters with his fellow students, both male and female,
and probably would not grieve if this relationship were
to end abruptly.

I suspect the continued use of mildly narcotic drugs,
including such illegal agents as "Spice," "Pink," and
"Harrolin." (No definite proof here.) Subject's manner
is lackadaisical and uncaring. Selfish, introverted, narcissistic. Typical T.A. major: more concerned with
things on a "higher plane" than with the exigencies of
everyday life.

Subject's strongest motivation for continuation of
education is the avoidance of the labor-draft.
RECOMMENDATION: 1-A status.

STATE OF CALIFORNIA, INFORMATION DUP-
OUT.
APPLICATION FOR CONTRACT TO ENTER
STATE OF LEGAL MARRIAGE
DATE: MAY 12, 2015
APPLICANTS:
DANA LEDGERTON DL 571-60-5683

PAUL-JOHN MURDOCK PJM 673-65-4532
LENGTH OF CONTRACT: THREE YEARS
PURPOSE: MUTUAL INTERDEPENDENCE
CONDITIONS: INDIVIDUAL PROPERTY MAIN-
TENANCE; DISSOLUTION TERMS NON-
NEGOTIABLE. MUTUAL INHERITANCE.
RESIDENCE: REAGAN HALL, UNIVERSITY OF
CALIFORNIA AT INDIO, ROOM 12-32
DISPOSITION OF APPLICATION: GRANTED.
WILLIAM APTHEKER, COUNTY CLERK.

HARDCOPY FRAGMENT IN FILE, dislocated page,
thought to be part of report by investigating agents.
(Nature of agency not known.)

"... *after his marriage broke up, he remained at the
University for another three years. He tried to reconcile
the contract several times, but twice he couldn't get in
touch with Paul-John and the third time, Paul-John was
vague in his reply.*

"*After that, he concentrated heavily on his studies.
He won a Ph.D. in bio-chemistry and an M.A. in medi-
cine. They were (in the words of the department head)
'Uninspired degrees'. Meaning he was qualified, but not
exceptional.*

"*Somehow he landed a teaching position and was able
to hold onto it for several years. They had him giving
the freshman science classes, something nobody else
wanted to do.*

"*What he did on his own time during those years is
beyond me, though I suspect he spent a lot of time at
the* artshows."

MAY 32, 2027
COLORADO COLLEGE OF SCIENCE
DENVER, COLORADO

FROM: *Dr. Margaret James-Mead*
TO: *Dept. Head Harlan Sloan*
Hal,

If I have to look at that "wispy little thing" wandering around the halls of this college one more day, I think I'll puke. You know who I mean. That man is a disgrace to the institution.

I don't care how you do it, but you've got to get rid of him. If you can't find something on him, make something. If you don't ask him for his resignation within a week, I'll give you mine instead.

Love, Maggie.

May 34, 2027
My dear Dr. Ledgerton,

It is with deepest regret that I must ask you to resign your position with the Denver College of Science. Your record here has been without blemish; however, we find that there is no longer any need for your services and are forced to take this rather unfortunate step.

I assure you that it has nothing to do with your personal life, or the incident with Dr. James-Mead. It is instead a question of . . .

MAY 3, 2029
INTERBEM CHEMICAL RESEARCH
PORTION OF SUPERVISOR'S REPORT

". . . the Ledgerton group seems to have come closest to a workable solution of this problem. They have generated an experimental strain, temporarily, designated NFK-98, which appears to combine the functions of both DFG-54 and DFS-09 into one continuous process, rather than the two separate steps we have today.

"Suggest further experimentation along these lines to substantiate the findings and put them into production. The Ledgerton group should be commended. Despite his unappealing appearance, Ledgerton is a tireless worker. Morale of the technicians working under him is not as good as it could be, but they do produce usable results.

"The viral research teams should be expanded as soon as possible in order to . . ."

INTERBEM CHEMICAL RESEARCH
MAY 9, 2029
TO ALL EMPLOYEES:
   COMPANY FACILITIES ARE NOT TO BE USED FOR PRIVATE RESEARCH PROJECTS WITHOUT FIRST SECURING PERMISSION FROM DEPARTMENT HEADS. IT IS UNDERSTOOD THAT INTERBEM RETAINS THE RIGHT OF FIRST OPTION ON ANY COMMERCIAL APPLICATION OF PRIVATE DISCOVERIES PRODUCED BY INTERBEM EMPLOYEES. REMEMBER, THIS PRIVILEGE IS CONDITIONAL UPON FULFILLMENT OF MINIMUM QUOTAS AND WILL BE REVOKED IF THEY ARE NOT MET.

MAY 1, 2030
FIRST DORIAN CHURCH OF AMERICA, OSCAR WILDE CONGREGATION, CONFIDENTIAL MEMBERSHIP REPORT:
   Dr. Dana Ledgerton, employee of InterBem Corporation, age thirty-six. Unmarried.
   Dr. Ledgerton was interviewed by the membership committee whose discussion follows. J.M. commented at length that Dr. Ledgerton is thirty-six and physically unappealing. He suggested that the only reason Ledgerton wants to join is because he cannot find sexual partners anywhere else.

K.R. found J.M.'s attitude and phrasing undignified and demeaning.

L.N. said that Ledgerton's primary purpose in joining the church is probably loneliness.

J.M. agreed, but said that loneliness was just another way of saying "horniness."

L.N. insisted that the applicant was basically good intentioned. Lots of people join churches because they are lonely. Why should the Dorians be any different.

K.R. interrupted both of them to speculate on whether or not Ledgerton really did embrace the principles of Dorianism.

Ledgerton was called back into the room then and further questioned. He responded at length and the discussion continued again, while he waited outside.

A.S., visiting minister from the bay area, cast his support in favor of Ledgerton. Most people, he said, are not aware of all the precepts of Dorianism when they join, and it would be unfair to hold that against Ledgerton.

A vote was taken then, and Ledgerton was admitted to the membership by a count of 4-1. He was readmitted to the room and sworn to uphold the church and the principles upon which it was founded, that overpopulation is a sin and that all Dorians will devote their whole lives to zero population growth.

Dr. Ledgerton will be presented to the general congregation at the next open meeting.

MAY 39, 2031
INTERBEM CHEMICAL RESEARCH
SUPPLY REQUISITION
Need: Forty hours' use of electron microscope for viral research. Private project. After hours use will be okay. Would appreciate available time as soon as possible.

(signed) D. Ledgerton

MAY 14, 2032
INTERBEM CHEMICAL RESEARCH
SUPERVISOR'S MEMO

Spoke to Ledgerton again today about his after-hours research. He's been working on this one project for nearly a year now, and he has spent nearly thirty-five thousand dollars on it. When questioned how much longer this line of research would continue, Ledgerton declined to say, but seemed to indicate that it would not be much longer.

I asked if he were close to a solution. He replied that he was closer to finding out that there was no solution, but would not go into any further detail. I suspect he does not want to discuss his project. A complete report on the objectives of his program and his findings has been ordered. He has until the end of the month to submit it, at which time it will be evaluated and decided whether or not he will be allowed to continue.

He was upset, but not as much as I expected. Perhaps he is nearing the end of his research after all. He mentioned something about a possible sabbatical later in the year. If he requests it, it is my recommendation that it be granted. His lapse in work has been only recent and may be due to personal problems. Ledgerton has always been a good worker, although his personal manner does leave something to be desired.

MAY 50, 2032
INTERBEM CHEMICAL RESEARCH
REQUEST FOR LEAVE OF ABSENCE
APPLICANT: DANA LEDGERTON DL 571 60
              5683
REASON: VACATION, INDEFINITE LENGTH
DISPOSITION OF APPLICATION: GRANTED

REMARKS: *(Scrawled in pen.) Good. I never liked him anyway.*

MAY 50, 2032
FIRST DORIAN CHURCH OF AMERICA, OSCAR WILDE CONGREGATION CONFIDENTIAL MEMBERSHIP REPORT:

The membership committee then considered a motion to expel D.L.

J.M. wanted to go on record as being opposed to D.L.'s membership in the first place. It was duly noted.

L.N. inquired as to what the charges against D.L. were.

J.M. said that D.L. has not been faithful to the principles upon which the credo is based.

K.R. noted that D.L. has been observed almost nightly in the company of "paid female prostitutes."

L.N. requested amplification of this charge.

J.M. presented receipts made out to D.L. from the Xanadu Pleasure Corp.

L.N. wanted to know how J.M. got the receipts, but he was ruled out of order. The issue at hand is D.L.'s transgressions, not J.M.'s source of information.

L.N. disagreed, saying that we should not be "spying on our brothers." He was ruled out of order again.

The vote was taken and D.L. was expelled by a count of 4-1. The general membership will be informed at the next open meeting.

MAY 7, 2036
FIRST DORIAN CHURCH OF AMERICA, OSCAR WILDE CONGREGATION CONFIDENTIAL MEMBERSHIP REPORT:

L.N. called the special meeting to order at 8:00 p.m. The first order of business was the reconsideration of the expulsion of D.L. four years ago. In light of recent *events, it has become obvious that D.L.'s actions at that time were not in violation of the basic principles of Dorianism.*

If anything, D.L., more than any other member, has done the most to further the cause of zero population growth.

K.R. noted some additional facts about the situation and a vote was taken. D.L. was unanimously readmitted to the congregation. He has not been notified because his whereabouts remain unknown.

It was decided not to apprise either the public or the general membership of this decision because of the adverse publicity this might bring to the church.

MAY 27, 2033
FILE: 639 RADZ
SUBMITTED BY: RESIDENT PHYSICIAN JAMES-TAYLOR RUGG

Mr. and Mrs. Robert D_____ came into my office on May 6 of this year. They have been trying for six months to start a baby and have had no success. I initiated the Groperson tests as well as a routine physical examination of each.

Mrs. D_____ is in excellent physical condition and well-suited for child-bearing. Mr. D_____ tests out with a normal sperm count and is in no need of semination-cloning. I'm sure that the rest of the tests will also turn out negative. I admit it, I'm stumped, and I pass this case on to the board with all the rest.

WRITTEN IN INK ACROSS THE BOTTOM: *Dammit! This is the twenty-third one of these I've seen in the past two months. What the hell is going on?*
(signed) B.V.

5-21-2033/TIMEFAX
... SURPRISINGLY, THE ONLY PLACE WHERE

THE POPULATION GROWTH HAS KEPT WITH-
IN ITS PROJECTED LIMITS HAS BEEN SOUTH-
ERN CALIFORNIA, THE DENSEST URBAN
COMPLEX IN THE COUNTRY. THE STATE SUR-
GEON GENERAL OFFERED NO EXPLANATION
FOR IT, BUT USED THE OCCASION TO CON-
DEMN ARTIFICIAL ADDITIVES IN THE YEAST-
CULTURES. HE NOTED AN INCREASE IN THE
NUMBER OF MARRIED COUPLES CONSULTING
DOCTORS ABOUT THEIR INABILITY TO CON-
CEIVE AND HINTED THAT THERE MIGHT BE
A CONNECTION.

IN CLEVELAND, DR. JOYCE FREMM' DIS-
COUNTED THIS, SUGGESTED INSTEAD THAT
THE CALIFORNIA SLOWDOWN WAS A RESULT
OF ITS BECOMING "ONE GIANT BEHAVIORAL
STINK." WHEN ASKED IF SHE DIDN'T MEAN
"BEHAVIORAL SINK," DR. FREMM REPLIED,
"I KNOW WHAT I SAID."

5-3-2034/TIMEFAX
CONCERN OVER THE SO-CALLED "INFERTILI-
TY PLAGUE" HAS SPREAD EVEN TO THE
EASTERN BLOC NATIONS. THE LATEST CITIES
TO REPORT DECLINING BIRTH RATES IN-
CLUDE MOSCOW, PEKING, HONG KONG, TO-
KYO, OSAKA, HANOI, NEW DELHI AND MEL-
BOURNE. EARLIER IN THE WEEK, THE PARIS
COUNCIL MET AGAIN TO REPORT STILL NO
SUCCESS IN FINDING THE CAUSE OF THE DE-
CLINE.

DR. JOYCE FREMM, WORKING OUT OF
SOUTHERN CALIFORNIA COMPLEX, UNIT
HOSPITAL 43, ADMITTED THAT HER TEAM
WAS NO CLOSER TO THE CAUSE THAN THEY
HAD BEEN A YEAR AGO. "ALL WE KNOW

ABOUT IT, WHATEVER IT IS," SHE SAID, "IS THAT IT KEEPS PEOPLE FROM STARTING BABIES."

SHE GAVE NO INDICATION WHEN A SOLUTION MIGHT BE FOUND. WHILE SHE WAS SPEAKING, THE W.H.O. RELEASED A LIST OF AN ADDITIONAL FOURTEEN NATIONS WHOSE BIRTH RATES HAVE BEGUN TO SHOW THE INITIAL SLOWING THAT INDICATES THE PRESENCE OF THE SYNDROME.

MAY 9, 2034
MEMO TO: DR. JOYCE FREMM
FROM: DR. VICTOR-WEBB KING
Joyce,

I don't know how important this is, but it wouldn't hurt to track it down. Out of the last three hundred couples I've interviewed, nearly sixty per cent of the men have met their wives and been married only in the past eighteen months. Out of this group, nearly half report occasional pre-marital visits to a joy house, and nearly a third of all the men we interviewed have had some kind of professional contact.

More important however, is that *at least one partner in every couple has had at least one pre- or extra-marital contact with a partner other than wife or husband*.

The former fact is way out of line with the statistical average; the latter implies a definite connection. Could the Xanadu Pleasure Corp be an active vector of the disease?

MAY 11, 2034
MEMO TO: DR. VICTOR-WEBB KING
FROM: DR. JOYCE FREMM

(1) We don't know yet that it's a disease.

(2) Make no public announcement of this—

especially do not suggest that Xanadu or any other company may be connected with it.

(3) Check it out immediately.

MAY 11, 2034
MEMO TO: DR. JOYCE FREMM
FROM: DR. CARLOS WAN-LEE
Dr. Fremm,

I believe my section has come up with a clue as to the nature of the syndrome. Sperm from one hundred affected men has been compared with the sperm of one hundred unaffected men; i.e. men whose wives have been impregnated within the past two months.

There is a minor but definite difference in the enzyme output of the affected sperm cells. All of the affected men (excepting three with very low sperm counts) had this qualitative difference in their enzyme production. Ninety-three of the unaffected men had normal enzyme production.

We're exploring this further and will have a more detailed report at the end of the week.

MAY 30, 2034
REPORT TO THE WORLD HEALTH ORGANIZATION BY DR. JOYCE FREMM
TRANSCRIPTION OF REMARKS—MOST CONFIDENTIAL
Gentlemen,

We have discovered the cause of the infertility plague, and we believe that it is only a matter of time until we discover the cure.

The cause of the plague is simple: We have been hit by a new kind of venereal disease—a benevolent tyrant, so to speak. It has an incubation period of less than twenty-four hours, and its immediate effects are so mild as to be negligible; perhaps a headache or a mild sense of nausea, that's all; but after that, the victim will pass the infection on to everyone he or she has intimate contact with.

Both males and females are carriers of the disease, creating an ever-increasing reservoir of active infection, with promiscuity its vector.

The disease has no effect on females of the species. To them, it is a benevolent parasite. It lives in the female reproductive tract and minds its own business. Unfortunately, its business is to infect that woman's every male contact.

And each time it does that, it effectively castrates the man. Viability of the sperm cells is reduced to 7% of what is considered normal.

The causative agent is a virus. It is a new strain and related to nothing we have seen before. Were it not for the fact that artificial virus tailoring is still such an infant science, I would suspect a vast campaign of virological warfare is being waged against the human race.

The viral bodies live and breed in the cells lining the vaginal wall. During intercourse, the release of certain hormones cause them to become active, and the viral bodies migrate into the male organ—usually through the urethra, but occasionally through a mild, almost unnoticeable rash.

The virus then migrates to the testes, specifically to the sperm-forming cells. The viral DNA chains attack these cells, burrowing into the cell walls, throwing off their protein sheaths and becoming just another hunk of DNA within the cell. Impossible to discover.

The result is small, very small—but very noticeable. The sperm cell no longer *"cares."*

The average human male ejaculation contains three hundred million sperm cells. Ideally, each of these cells has the capability of being *the* cell to fertilize the waiting egg; but after being infected by the virus, the quality of the whole ejaculation is changed. The sperm cells still race madly up the fallopian tubes to meet the ovum —but when they get there, they can't fertilize.

You see, each sperm cell carries a tiny amount of an enzyme called hyaluronidase. Hyaluronidase sub-one, that is. No matter what the enzyme is called, though— what does matter is that the virus changes the male so that he no longer produces that enzyme. Instead, he produces something else, some other enzyme. The virus adds a few little acids of its own to the amino chain of the enzyme, and instead of hyaluronidase$_1$ we get hyaluronidase$_2$—a very different creature altogether.

Hyaluronidase$_2$ is not as active as hyaluronidase$_1$. It takes longer to do its work. Much longer.

Although only one sperm cell is needed for fertilization to occur, three hundred million are provided in order that one will succeed. But because only one is needed, the other two million, nine hundred ninety-nine thousand, nine hundred and ninety nine sperm cells must be resisted. For that reason, the cell wall of the human ovum is too strong for any individual sperm cell to break down. Hyaluronidase is the enzyme that breaks down or softens the cell wall, and it takes the combined effort of all the sperm cells to provide enough of the enzyme to soften the wall enough for just one sperm cell to break through. Immediately upon fertilization, a change takes place in the cell wall to prevent other sperm cells from breaking in, a calculated resistance to their pressure.

But, if all those sperm cells are producing hyaluronidase$_2$ instead of hyaluronidase$_1$, fertilization will never take place at all. (Except in rare cases—too few to be considered.) The changed enzyme is still an enzyme, and it still works to soften the cell wall of the human egg—but it takes at least ten times longer to do it. And by that time, most of the sperm cells are already dead, dying, or too weak to complete the task of fertilization.

In addition, the ejaculation will also have introduced enough viral bodies into the woman so that if she weren't already, now she too will be infected and will pass the disease on to every subsequent male contact.

Insidious, isn't it?

Other than that, the virus has no effect at all on living human beings—only on the unborn. They stay that way. Unborn.

MAY 47, 2034
SUPPLEMENTARY REPORT, VIRT 897
W.H.O. FILE BVC 675
SUMMARY: The virus, designated VIRT 897, seems to have made its initial appearance on the western coast of the American continent in June or July of 2032, specifically in the area of the Southern California Urban Complex known as Angeles. (colloq. L.A. or "Ellay.") From there it migrated along the heaviest tourist routes, traveling eastward to Denver, St. Louis, Chicago, Dallas, Miami, and scattered parts of the eastern seaboard Urban Complex.

Within six months, it had also appeared and made its effects known in Seattle, Portland, Detroit, Pittsburgh and scattered areas surrounding. It extended the complete length of the western coast, being specifically virulent in Frisco and Diego counties, as well as in the areas already noted. It spread to Tia Juana, Mexico City and Acapulco. The same trend occurred simultaneously on the eastern coast, with scattered pockets of sterility spreading out from Boston, York, Jersey, Philadelphia and D.C. areas of the Urban Complex. Also affected were Toronto, Montreal and Quebec, as well as scattered areas surrounding.

At about the same time, it leapt both oceans simul-

taneously. Tracing the path of the falling birth rate,
the disease showed up in London, Paris, Rome, Berlin,
Warsaw, Munich, Belgrade, Dublin, Saigon, Seoul,
Hanoi, Tokyo, Okama, Osaka, Peking, Honolulu, Hong
Kong, Melbourne, Sidney, Buenos Aires, Caracas,
Panama City, Havana, and scattered points on the east
African Coast as well as in the Mediterranean and
Mid-East areas.

It is obvious that there are too many active vectors
by this time, making it increasingly difficult to trace the
spreading waves of infection. Not only does the disease
move too rapidly, but once the waves of infection over-
lap, their directions blur.

There is no way to tell at this time whether the
origin of the disease was deliberate or accidental or a
combination of both.

Detailed analysis charts are enclosed.

MAY 50, 2034
INTERBEM CHEMICAL RESEARCH
MEMO TO: DR. LEON K. HARGER
FROM: SECTION SUPERVISOR VANCE
Dr. Harger,

I've just finished reading the WHO report on the
sterility plague and a rather curious anomaly has caught
my eye. I'm forwarding it to you to see if you catch it
too. If you do, give me a buzz. If not, then forget I
said anything.

MAY 50, 2034
INTERBEM CHEMICAL RESEARCH
MEMO TO: ALL DEPARTMENTS
FROM: DR. LEON K. HARGER
Urgent! I need all data pertaining to Dr. Dana Ledger-
ton DL 571 60 5683 and any and all research that he
might have been involved in while he was employed

here. Also, anyone knowing his whereabouts or the itinerary of his sabbatical trip, please contact me immediately. I cannot understate the importance of this information!

MAY 1, 2035
TO: SUPREME COURT JUSTICE DOUGLAS
    JOSEPH WARREN
FROM: UNITED STATES ATTORNEY GENERAL
    ALFRED G. WYLER

Dear Doug,

This is strictly *off* the record, and you might want to burn this note after reading it.

I've been talking to the President, and he and I concur that it would be extremely unwise to allow the InterBem Company to be sued merely because Ledgerton was an employee of theirs at the time he constructed the Ledgerton Virus.

Yes, I've studied the briefs in the case. I know that the appealing lawyers make a good case for the company's negligence in not keeping tighter reins on their employees' after-hours research. They also make a good case that Ledgerton would have been unable to construct his artificial venereal disease without the company's research facilities.

However, no matter how good their case is, both the President and I agree that at this time it would be best for all parties if the appeal were turned down. The InterBem Company has been most cooperative with us in *every* area of our investigation, especially in our efforts to develop the artificial enzymes. To allow them to be sued now might destroy them as a viable corporation and would cost us a valuable ally in our fight against this thing.

I don't know if you're familiar with the fact, but my office has registered more than five hundred thou-

sand separate actions against Inter-Bem. That corporation can't afford to be embroiled in this kind of legal
piranhaism. If you allow this first appeal to be granted,
will be setting a dangerous precedent that might cost
the United States a valuable natural resource—i.e. a
commercially healthy corporation.

Yes, I know this smacks of pressuring, but this case
is too important to allow you to make a decision without knowing the administration's views on it. If you
have any questions, don't hesitate to call me.

(signed) Alfred

MAY 7, 2035
FROM: FIELD OPERATIVE JASON PETER
        GRIGG
TO: F.B.I. DIRECTOR WARREN J. HINDLER,
      HOOVER CENTER, WASHINGTON D.C.
FILE: DANA LEDGERTON, YTR 5683
Chief,

It's my guess that the Paul-John Murdock lead is
going to be another dead end and we'll probably have
to start digging backward. (I'll try to get up to Manweather Complex before the end of the month, though
I don't think I'm going to find much up there.)

We located Murdock in South Frisco, where he's
working as a shoe salesman. He has neither seen nor
heard of Ledgerton since their post-college days. Apparently, he doesn't miss him either. I get the impres-
sion that the only reason they married was so that
Murdock could avoid the labor-draft. The full inter-
view tape is enclosed.

On the other side of it, there's some evidence that
there was an emotional involvement on Ledgerton's part
and that he's been trying to contact Murdock, but without success. We'll continue to monitor Murdock on the
off chance that Ledgerton is still trying.

Oh, one more thing. The latest word on Ledgerton hints that he is somewhere in Africa and heading south. But I doubt it. Last week, he was in Scotland.

MAY 14, 2036
THE CONGRESSIONAL RECORD
CONGRESSMAN JOHN J. HOOKER; DEM, GEORGIA

Gentlemen, we are presented today with a unique opportunity. The development of the artificial enzyme insures that the human race will not die out—and it gives us the chance to end, once and for all, the population explosion.

We need not manufacture the enzyme indiscriminately, nor need we make it available to every member of the world's population. In fact, even if we wanted to, it would be beyond our technology to service twenty billion individuals.

We are not geared for rehabilitating the human race; we can only provide enough enzyme for a fraction of the people. Dr. Fremm has stated that even if we began a massive synthesis program right now, we would never be able to reach all of those who are infected.

According to Dr. Fremm and others, it is only a matter of time until every man, woman, and child on this planet has the disease. When that happens, the only people who will be able to procreate will be those to whom we provide the enzyme.

Gentlemen, I say to you—here is an opportunity we cannot pass up—historians will condemn us if we allow this golden moment to slip out of our grasp—the chance to optimize the human race, to remake humanity. Therefore, I wish at this time to introduce this bill which would give the government the right to withhold the enzyme from those individuals who are judged to have undesirable genes . . .

(The rest of Congressman Hooker's speech was drowned out.)

MAY 20, 2036
BERKELEY NEW PRESS:

> U.S. PLANS RACIAL WARFARE . . .
> Hooker (The Aardvark)'s plan would be
> only the first foot in the door. For instance,
> what would keep the establishment slime
> from declaring Negro-ness an "undesirable
> trait"?
>
> In cities across the nation, Freedom Now
> groups are planning urban disturbances to
> demonstrate their opposition to any form of
> "optimization," which would be only another
> word for genocide. The right to bear children
> is a right, not a privilege—and certainly not
> something that can be legislated. All right-
> thinking citizens are urged to come this week-
> end to the Free People's Plaza . . .

MAY 3, 2037
FROM: FIELD OPERATIVE JASON PETER
      GRIGG
TO: F.B.I. DIRECTOR WARREN J. HINDLER,
    HOOVER CENTER, WASHINGTON D.C.
FILE: LEDGERTON YTR 5683
Chief,

The monitor on Murdock has turned up an interesting postcard (fax herewith enclosed) postmarked
Brazil. Although there's no name signed to it, the
content and phrasing could be a code of some sort. Or
perhaps a reference to a personal experience known
only to Murdock and Ledgerton. It should be checked
out by one of our Brazilian operatives as soon as

possible. I would appreciate being kept informed on this lead.

5-9-2037/TIMEFAX
. . . THE RIOTERS FOCUSSED PARTICULARLY ON THE SYMBOLS OF ESTABLISHMENT CONTROL. FOUR BIRTH CONTROL CENTERS IN HARLEMTOWN WERE SACKED AS WELL AS ALL BUT ONE OF THE AREA'S TEN ENZYME CONTROL CLINICS. THIS OUTBREAK WAS THE WORST RIOTING TO HIT THE CITY IN SEVEN MONTHS, AND ACCORDING TO MAYOR GILBERT ROCKEFELLER, "IT DOES NOT LOOK AS IF THE END IS IN SIGHT."
MEANWHILE, IN WASHINGTONTOWN, THE PRESIDENT DEPLORED THE NATION'S GROWING TREND TO VIOLENCE AND PROMISED IMMEDIATE STEPS TO HALT IT IN THE FUTURE. WITH THAT, HE SIGNED INTO LAW THE CONTROVÉRSIAL MANPOWER CONTROL BILL . . .

5-11-2037/DATELINE:BRAZIL. RIO DE JANEIRO. PRESIDENT GARCIA TODAY ANNOUNCED THE CAPTURE OF THE NOTORIOUS RACE-CRIMINAL, DANA LEDGERTON (DL 571 60 5683) AT RIO DE JANEIRO AIRPORT. LEDGERTON WAS ATTEMPTING TO BOARD AN AFRICAN-BOUND FLIGHT WHEN BRAZILIAN AGENTS SCOOPED HIM UP. HE IS BEING HELD IN RIO INDEFINITELY.
THE BRAZILIAN GOVERNMENT HAS ANNOUNCED IT INTENDS TO TRY LEDGERTON FOR THE CRIME OF GENOCIDE, AS WELL AS OTHER CRIMES AGAINST HUMANITY. ANGRY CROWDS HAVE BEEN MILLING IN THE

STREETS OF RIO EVER SINCE THE AN-
NOUNCEMENT OF LEDGERTON'S CAPTURE
WAS MADE.
WORLDWIDE REACTION TO THE ANNOUNCE-
MENT WAS IMMEDIATE. IN THE UNITED
STATES, THE PRESIDENT SAID . . .

MAY 5, 2040
REPORT TO THE WORLD HEALTH ORGANIZA-
TION BY DR. JOYCE FREMM
MOST CONFIDENTIAL—TRANSCRIPTION OF
REMARKS
Gentlemen,

Our recent studies on the enzyme synthesis program
suggest that there is just no way to do what you ask—
at least not without massive appropriations—and I, for
one, am opposed to it.

(Pause)

If I may continue . . . . If I may continue . . . I'll
wait . . . .

If the delegate from Nairobi will stop calling me a
racist slime long enough to listen, I will explain my
position. Any appropriations for the enzyme synthesis
would have to be made at the expense of other programs
—and the amount of money needed to do what the
delegate from Nairobi wishes us to do would necessitate
the closing down of almost every other United Nations
Program now in existence, with the exception of the
pollution board. And the pollution board is far more
important than this!

If I may continue . . . . I believe that there is a way
to save the human race, but enzyme synthesis is not it.
In any case, a few years of minimal breeding will not
hurt this planet any. There are about nineteen and a
half billion too many people on Earth already.

5-11-2041/TIMEFAX
THE IRISH CIVIL WAR, WHICH HAS BEEN
SMOULDERING FOR MORE THAN TWENTY
YEARS, BURST INTO THE NEWS AGAIN TODAY
WITH THE BURNING OF DUBLIN. THE CATHO-
LIC FACTION IN IRELAND CONTINUES TO
CHARGE THAT THE NEO-PROTESTANT GOV-
ERNMENT IS WITHOLDING THE ENZYME
FROM CATHOLIC MOTHERS IN AN ATTEMPT
TO REDUCE THE NUMBER OF CATHOLICS IN
THE NATION. THAT CHARGE WAS ECHOED
ACROSS THE GLOBE BY OTHER MINORITIES
IN OTHER NATIONS. IN ISRAEL, THE ARAB
AND LEBANESE NATIONALS CHARGED THE
ISRAELI GOVERNMENT WITH DELIBERATE
BIRTHCRIMES. THE JEWISH MINORITY IN THE
SOVIET UNION LEVELED THE SAME CHARGE
AGAINST THE KREMLIN. THE CHINESE MI-
NORITIES IN MALAYSIA AND INDIA HAVE
ALSO CHARGED THOSE TWO GOVERNMENTS
WITH WITHOLDING THE ENZYME.
THIS BRINGS TO A TOTAL OF FORTY-THREE,
THE NUMBER OF COMPLAINTS REGISTERED
WITH THE V.N. MINORITY PROCREATION
CONTROL OFFICE.

MAY 19, 2041
TO: THE PRESIDENT OF THE UNITED STATES
FROM: WARREN J. HINDLER, HOOVER CEN-
          TER
Mr. President,

   The situation is becoming more and more serious
every day. I have reports coming across my desk that
indicate that the activists are planning to step up the
number of urban disturbances within the next two
months. This nation is headed for civil war unless some

way is found to take the steam out of the Anti-Enzyme movement.

I would like to recommend immediate action along the following lines . . . .

MAY 20, 2041
POLICE REPORT, MANWEATHER COMPLEX
At 7:45 pm, Officers J.G. and R.F. investigated a complaint at 1456 Rafferty Avenue, Block 12, Apt 56-789. Investigating Officers found Donald Ruddigore in process of assaulting his wife, Alice. Woman had already sustained minor injuries.

Ruddigore explained that his wife had told him she was pregnant. As he had been infected with the Ledgerton Virus some years earlier, he knew that he could not be the father of the child, and he had only begun beating her when she refused to tell him who the real father was.

When questioned, Mrs. Ruddigore insisted that she has never copulated with anyone but her husband. Officer G. Suggested that both Ruddigores see a County Clinician before the week was over.

Mr. Ruddigore became abusive at this and had to be forcibly restrained. He was booked at Station 12 (preventive detention) and released the following morning on his own recognizance. Mrs. Ruddigore spent the night at her sister's after being released from the Emergency Hospital, where she was treated for minor scalp injuries.

As he was being taken into custody, Mr. Ruddigore noted that he was "glad that whoever the bastard is, now he's got it too!"

MAY 38, 2041
TO: DR. JOYCE FREMM
FROM: DR. CARLOS WAN-LEE

Joyce,

I've had four physicians call me in the past two days wanting to know if someone is bootlegging enzyme or something. All of them report a number of women (with previously infected husbands) turning up unexpectedly pregnant. Yes, I know it sounds like adultery, but I suspect it is something more. I'd like to talk to you about it in detail. I think we should investigate this. Are you free for lunch?

5-14-2042/DATELINE:BRAZIL. IN RIO TODAY, A CROWD OF MORE THAN TEN THOUSAND FORMED IN FRONT OF THE LEDGERTON GAL-LOWS TO HOLD A MEMORIAL SERVICE FOR DANA LEDGERTON, WHO DIED FIVE YEARS AGO ON THIS SPOT. WHILE LEDGERTON'S NAME IS STILL REVILED IN MANY PARTS OF THE GLOBE, A GROWING NUMBER OF PEOPLE ARE BEGINNING TO REALIZE THAT NOT EVERY EFFECT OF THE LEDGERTON VIRUS IS NECESSARILY EVIL. THE BRAZILIAN BIRTH RATE, FOR EXAMPLE, HAS DROPPED TO A COMFORTABLE . . .

MAY 20, 2042
REPORT TO THE WORLD HEALTH ORGANIZA-TION BY DR. JOYCE FREMM
TRANSCRIPTION OF REMARKS—FOR PUBLIC RELEASE

. . . what has happened is this: The virus has mutated. It wasn't stable. Few viruses are.

We have, in the laboratories, taken the virus through a total of seven different mutations, each of which has a different effect on human fertility. At present, we have no way of stopping the virus completely, but if our early tests hold true, the human race will be able to stop worrying about its birth rate.

Ledgerton Virus sub-one reduces fertility to a scant 7%. Variety sub-two, which is currently sweeping the globe, raises that percentage to 53%. Certainly not what it was before, but high enough for two very determined people to start a baby, if they wish. The other varieties, which we've produced through careful bombardment of radiation (and other techniques), produce fertility levels ranging from 89% normal to 17%.

We can expect the virus to keep mutating at least once every four years. This is often enough to keep humanity from developing any kind of immunity to it. Also, it will hold the birth rate down, without keeping it dangerously depressed.

Gentlemen, without knowing it, Dr. Ledgerton seems to have stopped the population explosion.

MAY 43, 2045
TO: THE PRESIDENT OF THE UNITED STATES
FROM: THE SECRETARY OF INFORMATION
Mr. President,

Enclosed are samples of the publicity releases you requested.

You will note that we have taken great pains to minimize Ledgerton's homosexuality. As you said, "It wouldn't do to have an effeminate American hero."

Motivational Research indicates that the need for a new American hero is greater than ever now, especially since the recent Mexican defeat. For that reason, I urge that we initiate this program as soon as possible.

MAY 49, 2045
MINISTRY OF INFORMATION PAMPHLET
#354657-098

. . . Singlehandedly, this determined little man stopped the population explosion, stopped it dead with a biological brake—then he set that same brake so that it would release gently, allowing the race to maintain itself, but to cease its cancerous growth. When the death rates level off in the next few generations to match the new birth rates, the Earth will enjoy an era of peace and prosperity such as it has never known before . . . .

MAY 4, 2046
TO: THE SECRETARY OF FINANCE
FROM: THE PRESIDENT OF THE UNITED
*   STATES*

Dear Jase,

   Sorry, but I'm going to have to ask you to quash your economic report on the primary causes of the current depression.

   You're probably correct that the economy's continued growth is a direct factor of the nation's population spiral—but we can't suggest that fact publicly without starting a minor panic. (Besides, anything which would reflect negatively on the Ledgerton Program would not be welcome in certain circles.)

   I agree with your recommendations though, and if you will circulate copies of your report (privately) to the Vice President and to the Secretary of Commerce, and also to the Secretary of the Treasury, between us we can initiate some of the steps you recommend to keep our financial heads above water.

   And the sooner the better. This is an election year and we want to retain control of the House.

MAY 19, 2049
EXCERPT FROM *TODAY'S PSYCHOLOGY*

   . . . one of the effects is the disappearance of the term "unwanted child" from the language. There is no such thing any more as an unwanted child. All children are wanted. Just look at the crowd of adults standing by the fence at any playground today.

Of course, not all the cultural changes are so benefi- cent. For instance, in the past, the pregnancy of an un- married girl could quite likely have been the result of a mistake. Today, it can only be the result of several nights of steady "mistakes."

However, now that the onus of pregnancy has been removed from intercourse, certain other moral conven- tions are vanishing. Women are enjoying a sexual freedom even greater than that of the late twentieth century, when use of the oral contraceptive became widespread.

In general, the population of the nation is more birth-conscious than ever before, and one of the side effects has been a reduced tolerance for social and sexual deviants. Homosexuals have been driven out of several cities, and there is reason to believe that this trend will continue for some time . . . .

5-6-2050/TIMEFAX
. . . FOUND BEATEN TO DEATH IN AN ALLEY. THE MAN WAS LATER IDENTIFIED AS PAUL- JOHN MURDOCK, A VAGRANT. POLICE SUS- PECT THE BEATING DEATH IS JUST ONE MORE IN A SERIES OF "ANTI-FAGGOT" INCIDENTS THAT HAVE RACKED URBANA IN RECENT MONTHS.

5-10-2053/TIMEFAX
. . . THE PRESIDENT ANNOUNCED TODAY A NEW STAMP COMMEMORATING THE WORK OF DR. DANA LEDGERTON, CONSTRUCTOR OF THE FERTILITY VIRUS. THE STAMP WILL GO ON SALE IN FOUR DAYS, TIMED TO COINCIDE WITH THE SIXTEENTH ANNIVERSARY OF HIS DEATH . . . .

This Crystal Castle

It is night, and the plants are scratching at the walls of the castle, a horrible sibilant sound. And the vampires are out; I can hear them cawing their insatiable craving. During the day they sleep somewhere in the dark valley below; at night, the scent of fresh blood draws them up the mountain and they circle ceaselessly about the castle. With the first pink and yellow rays of the sun they will shrink back down into their unholy valley; but for now, they circle and moan.

The plants too are moaning. By day they take in oxygen, storing it in great flaccid sacs. In the cold night the sacs leak; the air seeps out in long meaningless groans, echoing the hunger of the vampires.

I stand before the great bronze doors of the castle and listen to the incessant scrabbling of the plants. Sometimes I want to throw back those heavy doors and open myself to the night and the creatures that inhabit it. I could if I wanted to. I could; I know I could. I think the servants might even let me.

Or maybe they wouldn't. Someday I'll find out.

At last morning comes bright through the castle windows, and I rush eagerly down the stairs leading from my chambers and burst out into the world. The morning is a blue and white color. Always there is a breeze. If there is any warmth from the sun, the wind will wash it away. The star is a hole in the sky, a yellow-white glare; bright and cold, it cannot banish the chill of this great looming mountain.

Today the flowers are red and yellow and they sparkle with little crystal droplets. Lovely they are, but lethal to touch. By noon they will have begun to wilt, and by afternoon they will be dead. By the time the sun nears the west there will be nothing left but shriveled wisps of meaningless ash.

I stay on the walks of glass; they sparkle too, but not with the dampness. Lovely they are too, but not lethal. Here and there are delicate black designs, like trapped insects imbedded in the crystal layers of the walk; the light is broken into sparkling shards. Beautiful.

Somewhere in the castle the servants are busying themselves with tasks of iron and crystal. I do not seek them, nor will they bother me. Here, high on the mountain, I am alone. I can see for miles. Down into a valley, deep-carpeted with trees of tall green and gold. At the bottom is a river, winding through the canyon— narrow looking from here, but actually wide to cross.

Then, up the other side of the rift, almost a solid straight wall of living green, at last giving way to the rocky tops across. And beyond are other mountains, sometimes shrouded in clouds, but more often with purpling peaks crisp against the sky.

The distance must be miles. There are no castles on the other peaks. I am alone, the lord of this land, the lonely lord of this land. This beautiful and empty land.

Like a grim dragon perched upon its towering aerie, the castle looms behind me. It looks over its world and broods, this great crystal and stone monster, glittering and glimmering in the light with sparks of white and gold and shimmery green.

Parapets and arching towers, lofty terraces and balconies—all perch delicately atop those forbidding walls. Too high, too high, all too high. The walls below remain unbroken. Not a window, not a chink in their crystal surfaces. Every night I can hear the plants scrabbling and scratching as they strain for purchase. But the walls are good walls. They separate things—the plants from me, and me from the world.

The castle is carved out of the mountain itself. Great stones have been cut from the heart and raised to form walls around the summit. It is as if the whole of the mountain is only the base of the spire and the castle its pinnacle. It must be beautiful from a distance.

My table is set, as always, in the garden—the garden that blooms at night and dies in the day. The service is crystal, as is everything in my world, even down to the utensils. The same type of crystal that walls the castle.

The bread is fresh. As always. The meat is red and spicy beneath its crystal cover, and a goblet glitters with promises of icy sweet and tartness.

When I finish, a servant comes, gleaming like bronze, golden in the sunlight. Without blemish and without expression. They are all like that; I cannot tell one from another. They provide for my needs, all of them.

He does not look at me, he never does, but goes about his tasks with a familiar efficiency. He handles the emptied dishes with no sign of either obeisance or distaste, no emotion at all; and placing them on his tray, he goes. His footfall leaves the crystal walk ringing like bells.

It is the same every morning.

I wander about the grounds, but a complete circuit takes less than ten minutes.

There are places where balconies pause like after-thoughts, overlooking the steep sides of the mountain —places where a piece of wall and floor and perhaps a crystal bench have been put so as to keep the castle from having an unfinished look. I could throw myself off from one of these places.

But they would stop me. They always do.

Every day it is the same.

I note how the flowers are already losing their glimmer. The lustre of life is fading and their creepers are shriveling off the edge of the walk. In the darkness of night those same creepers will return to scrape and scratch at my unyielding surfaces.

Finally, even though they are watching me, they know and I know it is inevitable. I follow the walk down to where it touches the edge of the creeping forest. And I stare hungrily into that aching and uneasy mass of green and black. Deep shimmering buds cluster up and down the tall trunks. I imagine I can see past them —past their sluggish tendrils, far past—down to where the tall trees give way to the lesser ones, the twisted ones, where convoluted vines twist and wind among the dark grasping limbs at the bottom.

I find myself longing for the sight of just one living thing. Anything. An animal, any animal; a small one would do—just a squirrel or even a bird. An insect perhaps. Something alive. I mean *really* alive, not the half-alive, leech-like creatures that infest the forest. I mean something really alive. Anything.

I can stand it no longer; I turn away and back toward the castle looming dark above me. It is haloed by its own shimmering outline. The crystal walls glitter with the light of the yellow sun, which from here is hidden behind that great bulk. The sky is aching and empty blue behind it.

Just one living thing, I ask. Just one living thing.

I am possessed by frenzy. I run screaming through the castle in madness.

But the chairs are too heavy to throw, the draperies too strong to tear, the windows too thick to shatter. And of objects that might be used as weapons, there are none. The servants saw to that a long time ago.

I run screaming through the castle; hoarse cries echo blankly off impassive faces. "How can you let me go on like this?!! This is madness! I must escape! I must be free of this! I must!"

I scrape at the glittering walls until my nails are bloody and useless. I hammer and claw at them, all the time sobbing, sobbing, and collapsing in a heap.

When I am through, the servants tend my wounds.

Every day it is the same.

Except—

—once. He was young. Innocent. The freshness of spring was still on his cheeks. His eyes were closed, his skin was pale, and his hair was plastered wetly on his forehead.

The servants ran their silent hands across his frame. Minimal injuries. He had suffered no broken bones in the crash; only the shock, nothing more. Somewhere out in the night, pieces of a steel needle still smouldered across a gashed hillside.

At my direction, they carried him upstairs. There is only one bedchamber in the castle. Mine. The builders of this magnificent palace hadn't expected that one day I would be entertaining a guest.

The youth was placed in the huge bed in the chamber at the top of the stairs.

I fell asleep in a chair watching him.

Morning, and he was awake. His pale eyes were wide

with curiosity. How long had he been lying there staring at me? I nodded to him, slowly.

"Who are you?" he asked.

"You don't know," I said.

He looked at me curiously. "No. Who are you?"

I smiled. I crossed to the window and threw it open.
Daylight, somehow gold and warm, streamed through it.
My actions were slow and deliberate; his eyes were on
me as I moved, and for the first time I realized how
truly friendly the morning could be.

I stretched, and it was a pleasure just to breathe.
Although the ache of sleeping in the chair had settled in
my bones, a few moments in the morning sun promised
to bake it out.

"You didn't answer my question," he said.

I grunted in reply. Noncommittal. Looking at him,
I asked, "Are you feeling all right?"

He nodded and tried to move. A sudden grimace
crossed his face. "Uh, maybe I guess not. I'm still a
little sore."

"That should heal quickly enough. The servants found
little to be concerned about when we brought you in
last night." I studied him thoughtfully. He could have
been twenty or twenty-five. Youth is resilient.

"Am I in the castle?"

I nodded.

He smiled. "I thought so."

"Why?"

"Where else could I be? Except for the jungle, this
world is empty. The only thing on it is the castle.
From the sky it's a glittering jewel. The sun sparkles off
it in a hundred different colors."

He looked at me curiously, a long time; his eyes were
bright. (Am I male or female, I wonder? It has been so
long since I have . . . Too long, too long.) "Who *are*

you?" he asked again. "What's the reason for all this . . . this . . . ?"

A shake of the head. He cannot know. Not yet, not yet. He must not know. The first person I have seen since . . . since . . . The first person I have seen in far too long; I cannot lose him. I will not lose him.

I threw open the door of the chamber. The servants, all of them, were standing there helplessly. There was confusion in their milling. They were, for the first time in my experience, confronted with a situation they could not understand. Suddenly there were two persons in a castle built only for one.

Yesterday, yesterday when the ship came screaming across the sky, they had responded to their primary patterning, responded to the ingrained command that a man must not be allowed to come to injury, to suffer pain, or to die. But today, that man is alive and in the castle. In the castle designed only for one, there are *two!* And there is nothing in their conditioning to help them cope with such a fact. There should be only one, but there are two!

I delight in their confusion. Two! There are two! It is ecstasy! Bitter ecstasy. There are two!

Their confusion hints at something I had long suspected but never known how to prove. Were I to stop and consider it, it might prove disturbing; but in the dazzling excitement of the morning, I paid no attention.

"Breakfast!" I demanded, and once more given purpose, the servants disappeared into the hallways and corridors of the castle. Their footsteps faded into silence.

When I turned back to the other, he was standing—a bit unsteady, but able to move without difficulty. I offered him a hand (for the first time I noticed how thin and wrinkled it was), but he waved it off. Together we moved down the stairs, and he watched in curiosity as I threw back the bolts and opened the great bronze doors. I had to explain to him about the night and the forest—he did not remember—and that led to an explanation of how we rescued him. He did not ask why.

Outside, he stared up at the castle. He bent to examine the crystal surface of the walk, ticked at it with a fingernail, then smiled in embarrassment at being so curious.

The table was set with the morning meal, but there was only one chair.

The servant came when I called. He stared at me uncomprehendingly; his eyes were blank lenses. "Breakfast," I demanded and indicated the table. Only one set of steaming covered dishes sat there.

The servant stepped forward, he hesitated confusedly, looked at me, then started to remove the plates already there.

"No," I cut him off. "Leave those."

He replaced them, straightened, hesitated again, wheeled on one foot—

"No. Don't leave. Bring another serving."

The servant looked at me—blank eyes, blank lenses. He shifted his feet unsteadily. *I delight in their confusion, do I?* I crossed to the flyer and led him over to the chair, forced him to sit. "Eat."

"But, I can't. This is your meal—"

"You need it more than me." To the servant, "Bring me breakfast. I have no meal, I have no chair." To the flyer, "Eat." He took a tentative bite of food.

Abruptly the servant moved. He made one last try to clear the table. *If this is not food, then it must be waste;* he reached for the plates. "No," I stopped him again. "That is to be left there. Now bring me a chair and a meal."

The golden figure hesitated again, its naked body gleaming. It was silent and its eyes were empty. Had I gotten through to it? Did it understand? What thoughts whirred through that crystal mind? Was it deciding that the other man, the other meal, were not to be considered at all, that they were beyond the scope of its existence? Was it remembering its primary function that I must be served?

Abruptly it turned and disappeared into the castle. I would soon find out.

With the servant gone, the flyer laid down his fork. "I'll wait. If he doesn't bring you a meal, we can share this."

I shook my head in annoyance. "No." Then, realizing my curtness, I softened my tone. "I'm sorry, but this must be established now. Please eat."

"Are you sure? I—"

"I'm sure," I smiled at him reassuringly. He was so young. He took another tentative bite.

He need not have worried. The servant was returning, and he was carrying a (Where had he found that?) second chair, a mate to the one already at the table. Another servant appeared with a table setting, followed by a third who bore a steaming covered tray.

I had won a small victory in my world; I had forced a change in the daily routine! Or had the flyer forced the change? No matter. Things *could* be changed. Not without effort, but they could be *changed*.

The day was bright, the sky was high and blue. We sat in a garden of death beside a crystal castle and shared a meal. The meat was red and spicy, the nectar clear and sweet. I ate, but it was difficult to do more than just sit and stare at this other, this beautiful other.

My thoughts must have shown in my face, for he asked, "Why are you smiling like that?"

It was a hard question to answer. How can you share loneliness? How can you tell someone that you are thankful simply for his existence? I would reach out and touch him, but would he understand? It would be only to reassure myself that this is not, after all, a dream.

Finally, I just said, "I'm happy. That's all. Just happy."

He looked back at me; his eyes were deep. A hint of a smile appeared on his face. It was uncertain, and he covered it by bending again to his meal.

Later, we walked in the garden and I showed him the grounds of the castle. He still did not understand yet what it was; thought instead that it was a luxurious palace; thought that *I* was *its* keeper.

We walked down to the edge of the forest and I showed him the night creepers and the poisonous flowers and told him how we had had to save him from all that. He kept wanting to touch the delicate pastel blossoms; it was as if he had never known fear or pain; several times I had to stop him. The danger of the night cannot be understated. When we turned away, his face was troubled.

The servant, as always, was waiting with water. Only one goblet, of course; they do not learn easily. We shared it. First I drank, then he, then I again. He finished it. Its frosty clarity still lingers in the mouth.

"You still haven't told me who you are," he said.

"Someday, I will. Someday. Or perhaps you will find out for yourself."

"Why not now?"

Hesitation. Then, "Because, first you must learn to trust me."

"You say that as if there's some reason I shouldn't."

A smile. "How do you know there isn't?"

He cocked his head thoughtfully, a beautiful gesture. Beautiful. "I don't, do I?" A pause. "So, who are you?"

"You're not listening."

"Uh uh," he grinned. "Who are you?"

His good nature was infectious, but . . . "You'll have to trust me."

"I do trust you. I don't know you well enough yet to have reason not to. But the more you refuse, the more I think that maybe I shouldn't."

That hurt, but maybe it was meant to. Do *I* trust *him? Do I trust him enough?* "I am a human being," I answered. "I have a human soul and a human body, and most of all, human feelings."

It was the wrong answer; I could see that he wasn't satisfied with it. But he smiled, forced himself to smile, and said, "That sounds very mysterious."

"I know. But trust me. Trust me." And that too was the wrong thing to say, the wrong thing. *Trust me until I learn how to trust myself.* It was a wall between us, growing ever thicker.

Oh, how I long to break it down, but I can't.

Can't? Or won't?

And there the matter rested.

We were in the tower, listening to the blue wind tinkling the crystal chimes, little slivers of light frozen and dancing in the afternoon sun. The breeze played at them in a song without melody or rhythm.

"Is this all there is to your life?" he asked.

"Isn't it enough? I have no worries, no cares. All my wants are provided for."

"Except companionship," he said.

"Except companionship," I had to agree. "But now that you are here . . ." His eyes grew troubled at that; I left the thought unfinished. Instead, I gestured to indicate the castle and the forest. "It *is* a paradise, you know."

He was standing at the window then, gazing out at the deep valley. When I said it, he looked back at me. "Oh?"

"Yes. There are no other human beings around to spoil it."

"And that makes it a paradise?"

"Shouldn't it? Other people are the source of all misery. Men are always trying to control other men. Nobody is ever content with his own piece of life; a man is always trying to impress himself onto others. Here, there are no others. I can be myself, freely, without the fear that anyone else will . . . force himself on me. I am protected."

"And of course," he said with that soft whimsy of his, "by the same token, they are protected from you."

"Of course," I agreed. "That's part of the reason for the castle."

He turned back to the window, murmuring something. The wind, white colored now, ran airy fingers through his hair, and for a moment his words were lost to it. I asked him to repeat what he had said. Still looking out the window, he raised his voice. "I said, 'it's no longer a paradise now.' Not by your definition."

A pause. "Why is that?"

He paused too. "Because I'm here."

"No," I corrected him. "I'm glad you're here."

He shook his head. "No. You said that people are always trying to force themselves upon other people. That applies to us too."

"But there are only two of us."

"It's enough. What's to keep me from trying to force my will upon you? Or vice versa?"

There was no answer to that. Instead, "Perhaps it isn't a paradise then. Or perhaps, perhaps we need to rethink our concepts of paradise. Perhaps paradise can't be paradise until you have someone to share it with." And perhaps my voice quavered as I said it.

He didn't answer. He just stared out the window at that deep black valley.

Dinner was the same problem as breakfast, a subtle reminder that, whether I want it or not, I do have power over him. It is I who control whether or not he eats. But this time, the servant was quicker to realize the solution. Perhaps they can be taught to accommodate two people instead of one.

"But if they can," he asked. "Will you? Would you willingly relinquish your power over me?"

"I don't *want* any power over you," I snapped back. "I've already had my fill of power over other human beings. It was enough. It was *more* than enough. I don't want it ever again."

"Oh, but you do," he said. *"You do."*

I lowered my fork. "Explain that."

"Your name. You won't tell me what your name is."

"So?"

"That's an attempt to control my actions. By limiting my knowledge."

I looked at him for a long moment. He was right, of course; his eyes were grim. At last, I broke away from that glance, concentrated instead on my meat.

Crystal tinkled against crystal. Except for that we ate in silence. The wall between us was perceptibly thicker. The silence was deafening. And it would continue until it became unbearable.

He broke it first. "You have a transmitter here, don't you?"

I shook my head, but he didn't notice.

He said, "I'd like to use it. I should try to get in touch with—"

"I'm sorry. There is no transmitter here."

He still didn't get it. "But, you must—"

"I'm sorry," I repeated. "There is no transmitter here. I thought you understood. There is no contact between this castle and anywhere else. Nothing. *Nothing at all.* We are cut off."

"But, how—? There must be—"

Again: "I'm sorry. There isn't."

"That can't be! How can I let them know that I'm still alive?"

"You can't," I whispered, but he didn't hear me.

"I must get back!" he insisted. "I can't stay here."

"I'm afraid you have no choice. Like it or not, you have joined me in exile."

"The servants! They must have some contact!" There was a growing desperation in his voice.

"No," I said. "They're even greater prisoners than I. Oh, for a while I suspected that they were watching me and secretly reporting my actions to someone far away, but that was only a self-indulgent bit of fantasy on my part. The servants are nowhere near that sophisticated. No . . . *they* don't care about me anymore, not a bit. They've sealed me off and forgotten me."

"How can you be so sure?"

"If I still had any doubts about it, the servants' actions this morning would have been enough to dispel them. The servants were confronted with a new situation, one they were not programmed to cope with. They can't figure things out too well by themselves. It's obvious that they had no higher authority to check with, else there would have been no problem obtaining the second meal. In fact, it would have already been there. And you probably would have been rescued by now, I'm quite sure of that. They wouldn't have wanted you to be—contaminated."

"But—when I don't return—"

"They have probably written you off already. The whole purpose of *this*—" and I indicated the castle, the mountain, the forest, the world, "— is that there should be *no contact*."

And this time, it sank in.

His eyes were wide, "But—but, how could you let

them——? How could you let yourself be so totally cut off from everything?" His face was a study in confusion.

"Think about it," I said. "Do you think I had any choice in the matter?"

Night came, and the castle began to glow—pale pink, violet and shimmering blue, sparks of gold and black. Together we sealed the great bronze doors, hiding ourselves in the bright light of our chambers, hiding from the angry dark that wheels and hawks outside. With the windows closed, the cries of the flying things are muted, almost but not quite silenced.

He followed me as I made my rounds, checking every great door and each black window. Even the balconies and terraces must be sealed. Although the servants had preceded me in this task, I would be unable to sleep until I also had checked. Even so, I still never feel safe in the night.

"The plants, are they really that deadly?"

I paused, I'd been running my hand up and down along a crystal seam. "Do you know that we are the only two warm-blooded creatures on this planet? If there are others, I've never seen them. Those things out there —the plants and the others—those things are hungry. Had they found a hole in your suit, we would have found only a rotting piece of meat."

"You braved the night, though."

"The servants did. I—I—couldn't. They wouldn't let me." I dropped my hand from the sill and the seam I had been inspecting. Once more we moved down the hall. "There are *things* out there. *Things.* I've never gotten a clear glimpse of them, but I know they're there." —He glanced nervously toward the window— "Oh, you can't see them from here. You have to go

out into the forest. Way out. There's something about
the castle they don't like; maybe it's the crystals. Anyway, they don't come near. They stay deep down
in the valley; you can sense them. Great things they are,
lumbering around in the dark. And silent. Silent. Never
a sound. Never. If anything, they are the absence of
sound. Great silences in the night." I found myself
repeating the words in morbid fascination and muttered
to a stop.

He was silent too.

We returned to the great chamber on the main floor
of the castle. A crystal jumble there gives off a vague
flickering glow—reds and yellows, pinks and oranges. It
is my pseudo-fireplace. I dare not have a real one because the castle cannot be opened at night even the
width of a chimney.

"My pressure suit," he said. "That had a radio in it.
Perhaps—"

I knew what he was about to say. "I'm sorry. I
should have thought of it sooner, but it's too late now.
The servants will have already destroyed it. It was contaminated, you know. Night-fungus spores. If something is neither alive nor made out of crystal, the servants will see it only as waste and they'll destroy it."

"But you could have stopped them?" He was almost
accusing.

I shook my head. "I could have *tried,* but I think it
would have been useless. They don't understand anything but simple commands. They're not here to obey
me, only to provide for my needs. Only my needs—"

I stopped in sudden realization. He looked at me.
Waiting for me to go on.

"—Perhaps that's why you're here. . . ." I said
slowly.

"Huh?" He frowned.

"Perhaps that's why they rescued you—because—

because I *need* companionship." The words were difficult to say.

"Go on—" In spite of himself, he had to hear it.

"They're keyed only to me—you saw that this morning. They respond to what I need physically—and emotionally too. They ignore everything else—maybe everybody else. If I hadn't *needed* you—they might have left you there in the wreck of your ship—"

He sat down slowly. His knuckles were white where they gripped the edge of the chair. He looked up at me. "Then in order for me to survive, I have to help protect your life. If you die—"

I sat down too. Not knowing what to say.

Our eyes were locked. "Control—" he breathed. "The ultimate control—"

"No—" I said. "No!" But even as I tried to reject it, I knew it was true. "It's *trust!* We have to trust—"

He shook his head. Refusal. I stared at him while he picked at the arm of his chair, as if troubled by its crystal feel. He was painfully aware of my presence, though his glance was downward; the tumbled light cast flickering shadows across his face.

How could I say it? What words—? He glanced up, our eyes met—

"What—what can I do?" I managed to ask.

"Who are you?" is his reply. His voice has the intensity of the insane.

". . . Do you trust me?"

"How can I?"

"You have no choice."

A nod, he lowers his head in assent. Then, "Do *you* trust *me?*"

A pause. "I don't know. I don't know. . . ."

"Do you want to?" There was pleading in his voice, a fear—not of the castle, nor of this world, but of me, of perhaps the thought that I might reject him, might refuse to feed him and shelter him, might even now at this very moment throw him out into the hungry night.

"All right. I'll tell you."

"Your name?"

"Everything. Anything." Who I am. Why this castle is here.

Just three syllables.

It is a slap across the face.

His eyes widened, first in shock, then in disbelief, in realization, at last in fear. "Oh no—you can't be. You can't be." He tries to deny what he already knows is true. "No, not you—your crime, it was . . . it was . . ."

My crime! It is always *my* crime!

Men believed me. They believed *in* me. They worshipped me. They called me a son of God! What kind of a crime is that? *They did it of their own free will!*

And yet, still they persist in calling it *my* crime, *my* crime—because it was *I* who tried to control *them.* It was *I,* they claim, who forced *my* beliefs upon *their* world. *I* tried to regulate *their* actions. That was my crime.

It made no difference, the thousands, the millions of other crimes that were committed in my name. The dark murders, the fiery genocides, the thundering wars, the exploitations and the countless soul-destroying enslavements of man upon man—these were all as nothing, as grains of sand compared to a granite mountain; these crimes were unimportant, hardly crimes at all. Mine was the worst. Mine was the initial offense. I had begun it; *I* was the source. I had tried to *control* the lives of others.

Hypocrisy piled upon hypocrisy. Not only did I try to influence the course of their actions—but I dared to do it in the name of God—I tried to save their souls! I tried to save them from themselves!

Is that so horrible?

Ah, yes. It is the worst of all possible crimes.

It made no difference whether I was right or not—nor does it make any difference that they gave their souls willingly—the crime was still mine because I let them do so.

I do not remember any more if I even believed in what I did.

They called me messiah, and for that I must pay.

So I am cut out of the body human—isolated, separated, placed apart. I am safe here; and they are safe too, protected from me, a shriveled wisp of a man who rots alone on a mountain.

Here in my castle I am protected from all temptations; not a warm-blooded creature in my world to seduce my attentions. Not a soul. Not a *soul!* I am surrounded by soulless servants. I will never taint again.

Or have I already tainted?

This pale and gibbering young man before me—have I defiled him merely by existing?

"Oh no! Oh no!" He repeats it over and over and over again, trying to deny what cannot be denied. This crystal castle, my prison, bears mute witness to the reality of my name, my horrible horrible name.

"Trust me, *please!* Trust me!"

But his fear is too great; he backs away, arms in front of him as if to ward me off, as if my very glance will steal and suck the essence of his life. "Please, oh please, let it not be true. Oh, please God . . . please . . ." He blubbers in meaningless words. "Oh, God, let me out. Let me out, dear God, dear God, rescue me, rescue me! Oh my God, my God, why me? Why? Why? Why *me?!!*"

Mute I stand, my mouth working over and over, forming words for which there are no sounds. "I won't hurt you, I won't. Just trust me! *Trust me!*" But it is a useless protest. Men trusted me once before. And I trusted them.

He continues to retreat, back, ever back, until he comes up against the great bronze doors, the doors of death. He is startled by their sudden presence behind him; he puts his hand back, reaching eager and desperate. He catches at the clasp.

"No!" It is a shout from me, fear and trembling. "Don't open that door!" I take quick steps toward him, but he—*MY GOD, WHY DO THEY ALWAYS MISINTERPRET?!!*—thinks I am coming after him. *Oh, God, I will not hurt you! Will you please let me help you!*

The plea is ignored. The bolt is pulled back even before the words have left my lips, and he is out into the night. I am running, running now, to the door, calling him to return. Screaming, I am screaming. Hoarse rage. Things batter at the bronze—black and leathery, with lidless eyes; red hate and desire—and I am pushing, pushing back the night. The vampires are shrieking; already some of them have gained entrance, whirling and flapping in the light, careening off the walls. And then, a final shove and the door is closed. Shut again to the night.

A vampire dives at me, hits the door with a thump, and slides weakly to the floor, still flapping. The light drains it of its fury. Trembling, I hang against the door, arms stretched out along the bolt. I must save him and I can't; I can't, I know I can't.

We are separated by more than just the door. The gulf is too big. I can no more save him than I could save those myriads of others who wouldn't believe in me. I can no more save him than I could save those who *did*.

Again, failure is the bitter taste of ashes. Were I what I once believed I was, what others believed I was, I would throw back these doors and go after that lost innocent. Instead, I tremble in fear, spread-eagled on a great crystal bolt.

I dare not go into the night. I can open neither the castle nor myself. I must and I cannot.

He is out there. I can hear him screaming. Oh my God. His screams go on for hours.

MY GOD, MY GOD! IS MY CRIME REALLY SO HORRIBLE THAT I MUST PAY FOR IT LIKE THIS? HOW MUCH MUST I ENDURE?!!

FATHER, FORGIVE ME!!

In the Deadlands

Step. . .

Step. . .

Step. . .

Twenty-three men.

Step. . .

Step. . .

Step. . .

And twenty-three uniforms
of coarse brown wool.

Step. . .

Step...

Step...

Walking,
in step,
into the deadlands.

i don't like the deadlands. i never have.

Step...

Step...

But i guess i'm not alone. Nobody likes the deadlands.
i don't think i've ever met anybody who *likes* the
deadlands.

Step...

The floor of the deadlands is
different.
It's like hollow brick. Walking into the deadlands is
like walking into an empty tomb.

Step...

They say that the deadlands floor has been baked
solid, but i don't see how. The temperature in the deadlands hardly ever goes above 80°.

They say that the deadlands floor is completely dry
—that there's no moisture in it at all.

But i always thought that when ground became completely dry that it turned to dust—that it needed moisture to hold it together.

i don't know. There's a lot of things that they say...

It's all wrong.
It is.
It sounds hollow. Maybe it is.
And it's the wrong color too. Ground should not be orange and black and all run together and mottled.
It should be soft and brown and
gritty with little rocks in it,
and things growing
and

Nothing grows,
and there's no sand. . .
not even dust.

You can walk out of the deadlands with the same shine on your boots as when you walked in.

You would think that there would be sand in great curving dunes sweeping slowly across the deadlands.
There should be.
But there isn't. The deadlands is barren.

No dunes,
no sand,
no dust.
Just the ground and the sky.

Step. . .

The deadlands sky is so deep it hurts.

i mean, it's empty.

179

Nobody looks at the sky in the deadlands.

There are no clouds in a deadlands sky. There never are.

Just that deep empty blue.

If you look at it long enough, it begins to seem like the sky is underneath you and the ground is above you

and that you're walking across a great rusty ceiling with nothing beneath you and any moment

you are going to miss a step

and slip

and fall

and go plummeting down endlessly into that deep empty sky, turning and twisting forever trying to grab onto something . . .

something that isn't there.

It never is.

Just that deep empty blueness.

i mean, it's empty.

But that's the way it is in the deadlands.

Empty.

Your eye searches for something to hang onto, but there isn't anything.

Except, of course, the great painful white of the sun.

They say that it used to be yellow—the sun, i mean. i don't know. You hear a lot of talk about the way it used to be.

Like *green*.

They say that there used to be a color called *green*. They say that all the plants were colored *green* . . .

180

the grass and the leaves and the trees and the bushes . . .
    all were *green*.
Not brown and orange and black
—but *green*.

Whatever that means.

i don't know. Maybe the stories are true.
Probably they're just folk tales.

Although, when you're in the deadlands, you can't
see how there ever was anything else *but* deadlands.
The deadlands is eternal.

i mean, if anything is eternal, the deadlands is.

Step. . .

There's no wind in the deadlands.
No. That's wrong.

There's no wind in the deadlands now.

Other times there is a wind.
Mostly, it's a hot breath on the back of your neck,
    but there are stories about the deadlands wind picking
a man up and carrying him off.

i guess the deadlands gets to you after a while . . .
that sky and that barren floor.
Funny thing about the floor. It's rutted from horizon
to horizon. It's pitted and creased and scarred.

Used. . .

Corrugated like a sheet of rusty iron.

181

In some places it's scored as evenly as if it were done by a machine.

Every step scrapes along the grooves of the deadlands floor.

The ruts are shallow and just about the width of a man's foot.

Your boots stick in them.

With every step you take, the deadlands catches and grabs at your feet.

Step...   (grab)

Step...   (grab)

Step...   (grab)

We've been walking for about an hour now. It's hard to tell. Not many of us have watches
and in the deadlands, time is frozen by a white staring sun.

Step...

i guess i said that i don't like the deadlands, but it bears repeating.

Some of the guys say that you get used to it, but i don't see how. i never have.

They say that the deadlands has a weird kind of beauty.

Actually, *beauty* is the wrong word.

It's not beauty. It's a kind of...

It's a kind of...

a kind of...

182

There is no word.

It's like a feeling,
an empty feeling,
like something quiet
waiting.

Step. . .

There are twenty-three of us on this patrol. There's
the commander and eleven *"two"*s.
Twenty-three men.
A double line, walking.

Step. . .

Step. . .

Step. . .

Eleven *"two"*s. They run us in "two"s because they
want us to each keep an eye on our other half.

Ha.

i don't think Carl and i have exchanged twelve
words total.

Step. . .

i don't know why they run the deadlands patrols
anyway. It seems foolish,
a waste of effort.

They say that it's to protect the borderlands from
attack
But nobody really expects anyone to mount an attack
across the deadlands.
Not really.

Of course, nobody really knows what's on the other side of it, either.

We don't even know that it has an *other* side.

i mean, nobody's ever seen it.

That is, nobody's ever seen it and come back across the deadlands to tell us about it.

But,
even if somebody did manage to cross the deadlands from the other side, we'd see them coming for a long time before they got to the borderlands. We'd see them from the balloons.

. . .i was up in a balloon once.

It was an anchored balloon—they all are now—but it was still a balloon. (The balloons have to be anchored; otherwise they go drifting into the deadlands.)

This was a long time ago, but you could see twenty . . .maybe thirty miles into the deadlands.

Strange. . .

We were high—really high.

We could look back to the west and see the gray roofs of Fort Borderlands and the gray barracks, and the distant village of thatched roofs, and the surrounding fields of brown and gray; and in the far distance, the black Eternal Mountains.

It was all
so distant,
so far away.

But on the east

the deadlands was close,
immediate.

It seemed to be so close
that you could step right out of the gondola
and onto its hard baked floor.

You could see every detail of its orange and black
surface.

so clear,
so solid.

You could see right down into the corrugations of
the deadlands floor,
shallow ruts in a mottled orange and black surface.

It was as if it was only a few feet away.

Later, i learned that it was an optical illusion.
What i saw was not the regular corrugations—the
ones you notice when you're on the ground—the ones
that catch and grab at your feet.
What it is, is that the deadlands is ridged—corrugated on a gigantic scale. Just as it is corrugated
with shallow troughs and crests only a few inches
wide, it is also corrugated with great troughs and crests
many yards wide,
sometimes many miles wide.
The floor curves so wide and so subtly that you can't
detect it, except from a balloon.

i wonder,
i wonder, if i got down on my hands and knees and
looked at the shallow ruts that are beneath my feet
right now...

185

If i looked very carefully at these corrugations,
                would i see
                even tinier grooves scored within them?
i wonder. . .

Anyway,
they say that that's what causes some of the weird
things in the deadlands—the wide corrugations.
Things like the horizon being only twenty yards away,
or twenty miles.
i mean, that's the logical explanation, isn't it?

Isn't it?

                        Step. . .

                        Step. . .

                        Step. . .

Sometimes i wonder why they run the deadlands
patrols.

i mean, they tell us why, but sometimes i wonder
anyway.

i mean, why?

What's it for?

Sometimes. . .

i think,

i think, maybe we're supposed to be sacrifices, sacrifices to the deadlands.

Like, if we're sacrificed to the deadlands it'll be appeased for a little while and won't want more.

So we go into the deadlands, deep into the deadlands, in case it wants us.

and if it doesn't
then we come out.

i don't like it. i don't like it at all.

But i don't have to like it. i only have to do it.

Step. . .

Nobody talks.

But then again, there's little to say.

Step. . .

Every step scrapes.

scrapes.

scrapes.

187

There are things in the deadlands.
Oh, they won't admit it, but there are

things.

You hear stories,
and once in a while a patrol doesn't come back.

Scrape.

When that happens—when a patrol doesn't come back—they never admit it. Instead they say that it's been transferred.
Sometimes, even, they really do transfer a patrol. As if to prove all the others.

Scrape.

But you hear stories.

One patrol is rumored to have found some bodies. They were the bodies of the lost 31st patrol. (That's one that they admit they lost—they can't deny that one.)

They say that they were just sitting and staring,
just sitting and staring,
as if they had all died at the same time.

Scrape.

They say that they were perfectly preserved. You could even recognize faces.

They were mummified
like so much irradiated meat.

188

Scrape.

They left them there.

Later, when they went back, they were gone.

Scrape.

Scrape.

Scrape.

Just the hard-baked and orange-black floor
and the bright empty sky
and the white staring sun.

Step. . .

Scrape.

i remember,
    when i was a kid—before i joined the patrol—we
used to have a farm.
    It was on the borderlands. On the outermost edge.
    It was during one of those times when the deadlands
was growing. It had already taken over the eastern part
of the farm.

    After dinner we used to sit out on the front porch,
just me and Pa.
    It wasn't a very big porch, but then it wasn't a
very big house. It was just an old wooden house.
    An unpainted gray house.

    It never did seem like home to me anyway,
                    just some place we were living,
probably because the deadlands was so close.

189

The wood was dead. i mean,
most houses—the wood is alive, you can feel it,
but our house, the wood was different—dead to the
touch. The whole house was gray and empty and hollow.
The walls were thin,
thin gray boards.

i guess the deadlands had already gotten to it by
then.

Anyway,
we would sit on the porch and look across into the
east field.
The deadlands had already taken it over by then,
and it was dying.
The whole east field was dying.
It was brown and starting to turn black,
                        black . . . with streaks of orange.
Already the ground was hard.

The crop was just a few scraggly ears of brown and
dying corn, hardly worth the trouble to pick.
Even if we had, we couldn't have sold any of it.
Nobody will buy anything grown on a borderlands farm.
It has too much of the taste of the deadlands in it.

So Pa and i would just sit and stare at that worth-
less brown corn.
The deadlands had ignored our fences. It just crossed
them like it didn't matter,
like they weren't there at all,
and pretty soon they weren't.

I'd go out there,
and they'd crumble at my touch.

The ground
where the deadlands had touched it
was already different.
Not dead. Not yet—

Just different,
empty.

Hardly even dusty.
Dry, kind of.

We'd lost this field to the deadlands just like we
had lost the others,
and probably just like we would lose all the rest.

Pa and i had tried everything.
We'd tried sprays and manures and colored lights and
radiations and sonics and prayers
and curses.
But the deadlands just grew into the east field with
never so much as a by-your-leave and there wasn't a
thing we could do about it.
i think that's what killed Pa,
the deadlands.

i joined the patrol later.

i remember,
when it used to get dark
and we would sit out on the porch,
we would listen.

we'd listen to the deadlands,
just listen.

We'd sit out there on that gray wooden porch and
watch as the eastern edge of the world grew dark.

A hot wind would come up out of the deadlands.

It would carry a sound with it.

It was a soft sound,

a faint sound,
and
we'd sit and listen to it.

There was something out there

it had a voice . . .
it sounded like—

a distant chorus,
a choir

singing,
moaning.

. . .it was a mournful sound,

dark and soft,
very faint
and faraway;

floating

just below the horizon,

the dark,
sharp horizon,

. . .something was there,

                              softly
                              keening.

Something is still there.

Something is out there.
                    waiting.
                        You can hear it

                        softly
                        keening to itself.

That's why i don't like the deadlands.
The sound it makes.

Pa used to say that it was voices.
Voices of all the people ever lost in the deadlands.

They're wailing.
They're far away, but they're wailing and you can
hear them,

                              softly.

They're not crying for help either...

They're calling for you to come join them.

At least, that's what Pa used to say.
Then he'd take another pull on his pipe and stare
off into the east.

The sky would slowly
                      193

grow deeper,
and darker

and we'd sit there
listening.

Pa and i would sit on the front porch
every evening,
        just looking at the east field
and listening.
Every evening.

We'd sit that way for a long time,
till long after the sun had slipped down behind us
        and it became too dark to see.

After a while,
i'd get up from where i sat on the steps and i'd
kiss Pa good night.
His face was rough and stubbly with whiskers. That's
what I remember about him. His face was rough and
stubbly.

Then i'd go upstairs and go to bed.
i'd slip into a thin cotton nightshirt and then between
the dry dusty sheets and i'd try to sleep.
i'd lay there feeling very thin and very cold . . . and
very naked and alone.

That's when the deadland would moan its loudest.

i remember,
lying in bed,
trying to sleep on a night
and the wailing would come out of the deadlands
like all the souls in Hell.

194

That's how Pa would describe it.
Like all the souls in Hell.

Far off loud
and insistent,

a soft and empty
calling
sound,

waiting,
below the horizon.

After a while Pa would come up to bed.

We only had the one bed.
Pa would sleep on his side and i'd sleep on my side.
Actually, it was Ma's side, but
Ma hadn't used it in a long time.
Ma followed a calf out into the deadlands one day.

Leastways, that's what Pa said when i asked.
i was too small to remember and Pa never told me
any more than that.

Anyway,
after a while Pa would come up to bed.

i wouldn't say anything.

He always tried to be quiet because he thought i was
asleep,
and i'd always try to be quiet because. . .

well, just because.

i guess i didn't want him to think i was scared.

Once, though. . .
it was a long time ago. . .
once,
        when the deadlands was particularly loud,
Pa got into bed. . .
        (and the bedsprings creaked)
i was shivering
and i guess whimpering a little bit too.

Pa put his arms about me and drew me close.
        He held me that way for a long time.

        A long long time.
        Like he was protecting.
i could feel the warmth of his strong old hands about
me

— i felt. . .funny. . .
like. . .
like. . .

like for once, i was a part of Pa.

        i am.
        i am a part of Pa.

And something else,
        i'm a part of Ma too.

i guess that was why he held onto me for such a
long time.
Because i'm a part of Ma too, and i was all he had
left of her.

196

After a while he pulled away from me,
moved over to his own side of the bed.

i fell asleep with the deadlands ringing in my ears.

The whole house would moan with it...
Like Pa said,
Like all the souls in Hell.
        If there is a Hell.

If there is a Hell, i'm not afraid of it.
Not after growing up with the deadlands.

Not after growing up with the gnawing fear that one
night while i would be lying in bed asleep and helpless,
the deadlands might just decide to grow a little bit and
take over the house and everything in it,

and then the next time the deadlands wailed,
it would be wailing with my voice too.

The deadlands is growing you know.
Oh, *they* won't admit it. *They* say that it's only
pulsing.
You know,
sometimes it gets bigger,
sometimes it gets smaller.

i don't believe it.

Neither does anybody else who lives on the borderlands.
Maybe it does get smaller,
but then when it gets bigger again,
        it gets a whole lot bigger.

Already, it's taken over where our farm used to be.

197

The house isn't there any more,
but i know where it was,
and it's not there any more.

They tell me that I'm wrong.
They say that that's not where the farm was.
        The farm was farther north,
        and it's still there.

But *they're* scared.
They don't want to admit that one night the house
just
    disappeared.
    Melted away.
    Nothing left.

No house.
No fences.
No fields.
Nothing.

Just the deadlands a little closer than before.

                Step. . .

                Scrape.

Deeper now in the deadlands,
following the ruts.
    The corrugations here are so even one can follow
them for miles.
    That's how we know where we are in the deadlands.
We can't use a compass.
    Compasses don't work in the deadlands.
    it's like they're dead. . .

lost all their magnetism,
        or something.

So,
we use the ruts as a guide.

If we pick a starting point on the borderlands edge
    and then follow one of the grooves in the deadlands
floor,
    we can almost always be sure that we are somewhere
in the deadlands along that certain line.

If we start somewhere else and follow another rut,
then we know that we are somewhere along that line.

And that's about as much as anyone ever knows.
i mean, about where they are in the deadlands.

Step...

Scrape.

i hope that this one will be uneventful. This patrol,
i mean. i hope we don't find anything.
    i've been lucky so far. i've never been on a patrol
where they found anything, but i've heard stories.

i heard one story...

about—

But it's supposed to be just a story.

i don't know.

We're probably five-six miles into the deadlands now.

We're supposed to go as far as we can.
The commander wants to make twenty today.

Step. . .

Scrape.

Man shouldn't be alone with his thoughts too long.
Least not in the deadlands anyway.
He starts thinking too many things.

About himself.
About his buddies.

i've heard about guys out in the deadlands who have
just turned and walked away from their patrols,
just stepped right over the horizon and disappeared
with never a word to their buddies
and nobody even noticed.

One patrol
didn't notice until they had gotten out of the deadlands altogether
that their commander was no longer with them.

He'd wandered out by himself a few days before.

Step. . .

Scrape.

The orange-black floor,
the white staring sun,
the deep dark sky.

Step. . .
200

Scrape.

Best to stay in a group in the deadlands.
Safer.

Thought about the City again.
City!

Not big, but the biggest i've ever seen.
i had forty-eight hours leave there when i finished
training,
    before i was assigned to the patrol.

            Had my first woman in the City.
            Did not enjoy it.

            No stimulation.

            The guys say i did not miss
            anything.

There's talk about the deadlands patrol,
about what it does to you.
They say it kills your drive.

When i say *they,* i don't mean the other guys in the
patrol.
    i mean other patrols.
    Not deadlands patrols.
    Other patrols.

Guys in the deadlands patrol don't talk about it.

i heard stories when i first joined the patrol.
The deadlands kills the sex urge.
The deadlands keeps you from enjoying a woman.

Could prove it by me.
Could prove it by this patrol.
Rarely hear guys talking about girls.
No pinups in barracks either.
No regulations against it. Just no pinups.

When i was younger, i heard that the greatest sensation in the world was being with a woman.

i don't believe it.

The greatest sensation in the world is sleep.
Much more satisfying.

Especially sleep with no dreams.
Dreams are disturbing.

Step. . .

Scrape.

Twenty-three men.
Commander and eleven "two"s.

Carl—my other half—is new to this patrol.
So am i.
We are the next to last "two" in the troop.
We say nothing to each other.

i would like to talk to Carl.
In the barracks anyway.

Have nothing to say to him though.

So i say nothing.

                    Step. . .

                    Scrape.

The deadlands makes you feel
more

            More intense.

Now,
i feel more of one thing than i have felt since Pa died.
i feel alone.

                    Step. . .

                    Scrape.

i do not like the deadlands,

        and we are walking deeper into it.

                    Step. . .

                    Scrape.

In the Deadlands

Later,
numb now,
cannot think.

Can only walk.

Stop for night.
Day turns off.

Night begins.
We huddle around the light.
Not the warmth,
the light.

Temperature is 70°.

Air seems hot,
heavy.

The other men are talking
small talk.

i want to talk too.
i want to talk to Carl.
i want to talk to someone,
anyone.
i want to talk very badly.

i don't know what i want to say.
But i want someone to say it to.

Want

                    to look at someone.

Want

                    to touch someone,
                    anyone.

                                        Carl?

                            Anyone.

Carl is the other half of our *two*. Supposed to be
my buddy.
He is not.
He is the buddy of the clique.

Every patrol has a clique. i am never in the clique.
Carl always is.

Carl and i are supposed to be
buddies.
We are not.

i have nobody to talk to.
i am alone.

i try to sleep.
The deadlands floor is hard,
                uncomfortable.

Faraway,
the deadlands croons

            tuneless
            a lullaby of lonely,

            a distant chorus,

            a mournful sound,
            of something

            faint and faraway,

waiting,
just below the horizon

crooning
tunelessly
                very softly
                very far away...

and this time there are words.
206

Always before, i could never make out the words.
Always before, i could never make out the tune.

                              too faint
                              too distant

          But this time...

          one word...

                              very soft

                    C o m e ...

                    C o m e ...

                    C o m e ...

That's all,
just

                    C o m e ...

The air is heavy,
the night is still

and something with icy feet is standing on my back.

207

In the Deadlands

Second day now.
i think it's the second day.
It could be the second year.
Or the second century.
Or the second ???

                More lonely.

Carl jokes with the others,
not me.
He does not ignore me,
he is just indifferent.

                More lonely.

Carl is one of those people who is in on everything.
He always knows what is happening. He is always
the first one to get the joke,
as much as anyone jokes in the deadlands patrol.

More quiet.

More like . . . funeral.
Muted.

Pa's funeral.
Nobody cried.
Nobody talked.
Nobody said anything at all.
Just sat.
Muted.
Muted like the deadlands patrol.

Don't know how deep we are now.
Day and a half?
Two days?
Two years?

We will march until we reach the tortured rocks.
Then we will turn back.

It's two days march.
Maybe three.

Or four.
Or six.
Each time we march to the rocks it's different

Step. . .

Scrape.

i never prayed.
Never.
If i did pray though, i know what i'd pray for.
A safe comeback.

> To what?
> To Fort Borderlands?

Gray barracks. Gray grass. Gray flag. Gray food.
Gray everything. Gray. Everything gray.
Too gray.

> In the distance
> is the first of the tortured rocks
> > waiting.

The rocks are sized like men.
Some are big men, some are small men,
some are children.

> They're all kinds of twisted
> shapes.

This is where they were supposed to have found the
lost 31st patrol.

> About twenty feet inside
> the tortured rocks.

i suppose they must have wandered around until
they ran out of water.
Then they sat down to die.

They say that when a patrol gets lost in the deadlands
it's because they tried to cross the tortured rocks. Once
they go in, they don't come out.

They get confused
and can't tell which way they came.
They could be twenty feet from the edge of the
tortured rocks
and not know it.

The rocks are closer now.

Shouldn't look at them for too long.
They start to remind you
of things,

or people.

Obscene shapes
doing obscene things.

i once saw a rock that looked
like
two people embracing.
A man and a woman?
Two men?

Disturbing.

Disturbing because,
reminded me of two men i once knew. They had
disappeared in the deadlands.

tortured

twisted

frozen

petrified

i looked away.

211

Above,
the sun is a pinpoint of white hate

no heat

no warmth

In the deadlands the sun radiates death.

We're closer to the tortured rocks now. i can see
why you would lose your way.
They grow right out of the deadlands floor.

writhing
scarred with blacks and reds.

You can't see more than ten feet into the tortured
rocks.

You can't walk more than ten feet in a straight line
into the tortured rocks.
After twenty feet or so, you're lost.

Funny shapes among those
rocks.

There's one that looks like Pa.

Could be.

The deadlands swallowed up his
grave when it took the house.

In the Deadlands

i guess the deadlands gets to you after a while.

They say that there are sand dunes inside the tortured
rocks.
The wind blows the sand into the deadlands,
and it's caught by the tortured rocks.

They say that the rocks have been carved out by the
persistent grinding of the wind, and that's what gives
them their agonized shapes.

They're about a hundred yards away.

It's the commander's intention to go into the rocks
this time.

Dumb.

There is a different set of God in the deadlands.

We're closer to the rocks now.

We can see how the potholes and pits become deeper and more jagged.
We can see how the rocks grow out of the deadlands floor.

All the ruts lead to the tortured rocks.
Nobody knows if the tortured rocks cover only a few acres, or hundreds of miles.
There may even be several areas of tortured rocks.

Nobody knows.
You can't map the deadlands.

One patrol thought that the rocks were only a few acres, or at most a few miles.
They decided to walk around them.
We are still waiting for them to return.

That was twenty years ago.

We are going into the rocks now.
The commander has a length of cord. Every ten feet there is a knot in it.
He loops one end of it around a rock.

The rock is grotesque
        hunched over
        deformed
        twisted

The commander loops the cord around it

and we go in.

Clambering over one another,
stumbling through agonized

shapes of stones,
shards of souls,

        shattered,
        frozen

in a writhe
of torment.

Across crevices of fear and
        through corridors of pain

The wind picks up in intensity.
It whistles through the rocks.

        It shrieks.
        The rocks scrape at the entrails of the wind
                        and it shrieks.

The sun falls into the night behind us.

        Darkness.

        Only the whistling of the wind,

                                        the moaning
                                        of an injured beast,

We sit in a circle.

The light is in the center, a silent beacon
slowly revolving
casting agonized shadows
                        of the rocks closest to us
onto the twisted souls of the ones farther back.

                    Darkness beyond.

There is little talk.
A few of the men smoke
                    cigarettes like tiny eyes in the night.

We are five hundred yards into the tortured rocks.
We could be twenty miles.
Or twenty feet.
It's all the same.

                    The wind subsides

                    and changes

                    and picks up a new note,
216

a mournful note,

a keening,

a wail of something. . .

                    something
                    large
                    and watchful,
                    waiting,

                    biding its time,
                    crooning to itself.

The ground is hard and uneven.
Sleep is troubled.

In the Deadlands

We are coming out now.
Thank your own private gods.

According to the cord we are five hundred yards
into the tortured rocks.
And now we are coming out.

The commander winds up the cord as he walks.
Every ten feet he winds up another knot. We will
wind up a total of one hundred and fifty knots.

We struggle back the way we came, following the
twistings and turnings of the aching cord,
  clambering over one another,
                                sliding and scraping,
  pathetic in our eagerness to escape.

The rocks are red and yellow and black.
They arch and twist with painful frenzy.
They reach out with sharp plucking edges
to scratch and claw
                    the tender flesh.

The floor
is uneven and gouged.
Ridges protrude
at obscene angles,
and crevices sink away into bottomless abysses.

                        and i can feel
                        a warm hungry presence,
                        an enveloping
                        throbbing
                        flood of. . .

The commander winds up thirty knots.

We go on
in wordless agony.

The only sound
is the scraping of boots
across rock,
and wordless
        grunts of pain
as rock scrapes across flesh.

The sound is hideous.

Like a giant crab scrabbling across rocks and gasping for breath with deep rasping sighs.
Far off
in the distance,

i can hear him
clicking his mandibles
and tapping at the rocks with his claws
      as he comes clabbering after us.

               A cold taste of lonely. . .
               a sense of longing
               for that hot throbbing
               presence.

The commander winds up sixty knots.

We stumble and stagger—
the floor catches and grabs
and tries to trip.

The rocks turn and twist.
They scratch
and cut
and slash.

The sun hates with a fury,
The orb has become an eye of sleeting agony.
a white stare of deadly bright.

Invisible radiation lacerates our bodies.
The orb has become an eye of sleeting agony.
The senses are seared by it.

               and the warm
               amniotic presence
               radiates stronger.

The commander winds up ninety knots.

All the senses
scream for release.

White hot agony.
The flesh is seared.
The ears scream.
The eyes burn.

Flesh
is torn
away
from flesh.

Living tissue
dissolves
in pain.

The rocks rip and tear and grind.
The soul writhes.

                    A funny taste,
                    a funny flat taste
                    like metal.

The commander winds up one hundred and ten
knots.

                    It floods warm and cool
                           through me,

                    like wine.
                    Soul wine.

A whimpering
sound of fear,
something
crying for release.

Twenty-three molten agonies.
Twenty-three fear-stained souls.

Far away
something beats its mandibles in delight.

An immense weight
of terror,
a rasping in the lungs,
a pounding in the ears,
in the heart,
in the soul,
a throbbing in the flesh,
a pulsing stinging agony.

                    It floods down my throat,
                    down
                    and into my belly,
                    where it radiates
                    warmness
                    coolness
                    release
                    satisfaction
                    fulfillment,

i am six feet of burning, turning, twisting.
i am molten lava.
i am seared rock.

The soul shrieks soundlessly.
i am scraped raw.

The commander winds up one hundred and thirty
knots.

                              and slowly
                              it permeates my body,
                              pulsing
                              outward   through   my
                              flesh,
                              something warm
                              and hungry and thirsting,
                              and i am warm
                              and hungry
                              and thirsting

and i whimper.
i shrink gibbering inside myself,
a quivering gobbet of flesh,

                    falling. . .

                    bending. . .

                    curling. . .

                    knees to chest.

Hands clenched in little pink
fists.

Fists to chin.
Head to knees.
Eyes tight.

Shoulders tight.
Elbows stiff.

And i am a ball of gibbering
fear.

    and i am released
    and satisfied
    and fulfilled.

A whimpering fetus,
shivering
quivering.

    i am fulfilled.

Clinging.
Must not let go.

The mouth works in silent
desire.
Imploring.
A red and white-hot burning
grows deep within the groin.

    i am fulfilled.

Rivulets of icy sweat
streak the tightened flesh.

i am fulfilled.
Do you understand that?
i am fulfilled!

NO!

We are fulfilled!
We are fulfilled!

Flesh,
chafed and scalded
and scraped raw,
bleeding from wounds too small
to see.

Searing air
rasps the throat
and burns the lungs.

All of us!
together!
We are fulfilled!

Somewhere a voice calls out,

One hundred and forty knots.

Far away is something big.
Something that scrabbles mindlessly,
clicking and ticking
and clattering across the deadlands floor.

Something that utters deep leathery groans
of slavering anticipation.

Chitinous claws scrape rock.
And fear
must un-knot me.

Fear must un-knot me.

> Slowly,
> a fist
> unclenches,
> becomes
> a claw,
> a hand.

> but we are fulfilled. . .

> Now
> the other one,
> slowly,
> slowly. . .

> We are fulfilled
> with an overpowering
> need
> and love

> Put
> one hand
> in front of the other

> love. . .
> (desire)

and
bring your head up.

     for each other
     and for the commander
     and

Put
one knee
in front of the other
and
ignore
the bloody flowing
from scraped and stinging
hands and knees.

     for Carl
     and for me too
     and

Crawl.

Crawl.

Crawl.

CRAWL, YOU SHIVERING BASTARD

One hand.

Now the other...

One knee.

Now the other...

And whimper.

       the deadlands
       and the rocks
       —especially the rocks—
       the warm embracing
       rocks,

Scraping
over jagged rocks,

flesh
is torn from flesh,

limb
is torn from limb,

entrails shattered
in a gutted belly.

       we are fulfilled
       and the warmth

floods through us
right up to the
top of our very being
and

BUT KEEP CRAWLING

Every living cell

screams

in white searing agony,

writhing

and burning

and turning

and twisting

and dissolving

into gobbets of terror...

Put one hand in front of you.

There, where you can see it.

Now, the other...

Now a knee,

a knee. . .

MOVE THAT KNEE

Look down.

Deep rasping breath.

And move that knee.

> i scream in defiance
> of all that is holy.

OH MY DEAR GOD IN HEAVEN

It is more than human flesh can stand.

i am rooted to the floor

and slowly

my cells must crystallize

and my limbs

must stiffen

and i must become

one of t h e l i v i n g

t o r t u r e d

One hundred and fifty knots.
And out.

Is it somewhere
something
howls in defeat?

In the Deadlands

i lie here on the deadlands floor
gasping for breath.

> *We* are me again
> with a cold bright clarity.

Nerve ends tingle
marvelling at unbroken flesh.

Clawed hands scratch futilely at the rock.
Unnecessarily,
for i am out.

> *We* become aware
> of my body
> here on the deadlands floor.

Deep rasping gasping breaths.
Sweet silence in the soul.

Only the sound of my lungs
sucking in air
and blowing it out again.

After a bit i raise my head.

i stagger to my feet
and

                         No.
                         Something is wrong.

                         We are confused.
                         We shake my head to clear it.

There.
That's better.

I am me again.
I am separate from them again.

I am unchanged.

It is time to go,
time to leave the deadlands.

I move out.

> Step. . .

> Step. . .

> Step. . .

Every step sounds hollow.
And more than hollow.
Every step echoes.

I walk on,
leaving the deadlands.

> The deadlands floor
> is hot and wasted,
> spattered with the color of
> blood.

> The deadlands sky
> is empty and unfeeling.
> The sun is implacable.

The deadlands floor is pitted and gouged and scarred.
It catches and grabs, but
I am walking out of the deadlands.

> Step. . .

Step...

Step...

The sun
is high and bright and cold.

And there is a presence,

> silent,
> dark,
> tuneless and brooding.

It envelops
hotly.
It throbs
and pulses.

It radiates
a warm sense of...
belonging,
and touches.

> a cold taste of lonely...
> desire
> for that hot throbbing
> something.

I stare into the empty east.

Far beyond the horizon
is something

                              faint and faraway,
                              softly
                              crooning.

        I wish I could remember what it is.

After a bit,
I turn.
I turn to the west.
I begin walking out.

                Out.

                Out.

Out of the deadlands.

Out.

I am coming out.

Out.
I am coming out of the deadlands.

Out.

And a distant chorus
Cries . . .

Follow the crease in the deadlands floor.

And run

run

run

run   as hard as you can

run   as fast as you can

run   Get as far away as you can.

run

run

From out of the deadlands

run

        comes

        a softly keening

run

voice of something

run

        faint and faraway

        something

run

        dark and brooding

run

        And run.

run

        Run.

run

run

run

run

run

run

run   One foot in front of the other.

run   That's all that's important.

run   Just keep putting one foot in front of the
other.

run
           The deadlands calls

run

run
                        C o m e . . .

run

run
                        C o m e . . .

run

run
                        C o m e . . .

run

run

run

run

run
           It calls with ten thousand thou-
sand voices.

run
           Too many voices
run
           that I know too well.

241

run

run

Come...

run

Come...

run

run

It is not a call.

run

It is not a beckoning.

run

It is not even a warning.

run

run

The deadlands is not calling me
to come to it...

run

run

No.
It is saying it will come to me.

run

run

Run.

run

Run for your life,
for your soul.

run

run

242

run
run
run
run   But run.
run
run
run
run

run   Something
run
run   lives in the deadlands.
run
run   Something
run
run   big.
run
run
run
run   Some day
run
run   it's going to get tired
run
run   of all the
run
run   little sacrifices
run
run   that we keep
run
run   making
run
run   to it.
run
run
run
run
run

run
run
run
run
run
run
run   Some day
run
run   that *something*
run
run   is going
run
run   to
run
run   come out of the deadlands.
run
run
run
run
run
run
run
run
run
run   Some day
run
run   something
run
run   is coming out of the deadlands.
run
run
run
run
run
run
run

run
run
run
run
run
run   Something is coming out of the
run   deadlands.
run
run
run
run
run
run   Run
run
run
run
run
run
run   Run
run
run
run
run
run
run
run
run
run
run
run
run
run
run
run
run

RECENT SELECTIONS FROM THE PUBLISHER OF THE BEST SCIENCE FICTION IN THE WORLD